LOOKING BEHIND

the gaseous life of a gastroenterologist

stories & poems

DAVID MARGOLIS MD

Uranus Publishing Company LLC
Saint Louis, MO

Published in the United States by Uranus Publishing Company LLC
Saint Louis, MO

This is a work of fiction, humorous essays and poems. Other than material directly relating to the author's experiences, any resemblance to actual events or locales or persons, living or dead, is merely coincidental, and names, characters, places, and incidents are either the products of the author's imagination or are used fictitiously.

Cover by Kristina Blank Makansi, Treehouse Publishing Group, LLC

ISBN: 978-0-9912154-0-9

Dedicated to my loving parents, Jack and Vera

Contents

** previously published story*

LOOKING BEHIND

the gaseous life of a gastroenterologist

Elmo's Story

My dog Elmo passed away this week. Elmo was a unique dog. He only liked people. The outdoors was not for him. He was an indoor dog. He did not care about chasing rabbits, the scent of other dogs, or going for a run. He wanted to be inside at a controlled temperature. It was as if he had lost all the primordial wolf genes.

We first met Elmo at the breeder's farm owned by Mr. Melvin Smith. As a practicing gastroenterologist, I had treated Mr. Smith for a bleeding ulcer a few years previously. At that time, we got to talking about dogs, and Mr. Smith told me I should look him up if we were ever interested in acquiring a standard poodle. Elmo was much larger than the other puppies there, and we found out from Mr. Smith that he was from an earlier litter. The first owners had brought him back because he could not be housebroken. Even though he appeared to be hyperactive, I immediately felt sorry for him and suggested to my wife that we take him in. The fifty percent discount from the price of the other dogs was also an enticement.

Elmo immediately became part of the family, and we soon realized that he had exceptional qualities. He loved to play with his stuffed toys. He would prance around the house, throwing them up in the air and then catching them back in his mouth. When he was given a new one, he would carefully place it on the carpet in the corner of the family room. Several days would pass before he would start to play with it. I eventually figured out that he wanted the new object to acquire the scent of the house. He needed it to marinate for a few days.

Elmo was an avid TV watcher. He liked to sit on a sofa with me and look at the screen. One exception was the theme music to the *Golden Girls*. This enraged him, and he would charge the TV set, barking wildly. We soon learned not to watch that show. He was also offended by my yelling at the TV during Sunday afternoon NFL games. He would take personal offence to that and slink away to another room until the game was over.

In his younger days he went to doggie day camp and became a celebrity there. We later found out that he didn't play with the other dogs, but sat with the counselors all day begging for treats. He knew the exact route to the place and would sit in the back seat directly behind my wife. If the car would go in a different direction, he would immediately start to whine with frequent, high-pitched yips.

As Elmo got older, he became more finicky. He slept on a doggie bed but had a regular human pillow (what else?) against the wall to rest his head. If that pillow became dislodged even slightly from its usual placement, he would whine and not lie down until we would fix it for him.

Last year, we noticed Elmo was beginning to fail. He developed weakness in his hind legs and had difficulty jumping up on the sofa. He had stopped playing with his toys. At about this time, I was consulted to see Mr. Smith again. Unfortunately Mr. Smith had suffered a stroke and had difficulty swallowing, and I was asked by his primary physician to place a feeding tube. His eyes lit up when I mentioned Elmo, but he was unable to speak. I thought his prognosis was uncertain, but both his wife and daughter thought there was a chance he could improve and eventually swallow again. The following day, I inserted the tube, and Mr. Smith was discharged to the nursing home.

Six weeks ago, Elmo developed pneumonia, and our vet thought a tumor might be present in his lung as well. He had lost weight and become incontinent of urine and stool, and we knew we would soon have to make the difficult decision of putting Elmo to sleep.

Mr. Smith was readmitted to the hospital last week, and I was called again to see him. Since our last visit about a year ago, he had developed kidney failure and had been placed on dialysis. He had become progressively more confused, and the feeding tube was never removed. This time he had been admitted to the intensive care unit in respiratory failure and placed on a ventilator. His abdomen had become distended, and a CT scan showed an abrupt decrease in the blood flow to his intestines. He was sedated and did not recognize me. I visited the family in the waiting room and explained to them that he would require emergent surgery, but his chances of surviving the operation were poor. I suggested that they consider hospice care to keep him comfortable in his final hours.

The following day, with heavy hearts, we loaded Elmo into the van for one last trip to our vet. So it was with great sadness that we said goodbye to Elmo last week. He went away with dignity and even managed to eat several treats at the vet's office before we put him down. I know in my lifetime I will never have another companion like Elmo, for he was truly my best friend. Before I left the hospital to pick up Elmo for his last ride, I passed Mr. Smith lying on a stretcher in the hallway. He was on his way to the operating room.

A Visit to the Doctor

Sorry I'm late, but I had to get all seventeen of my medicines together and put them in this grocery bag. Whoops, I guess there was a hole in the bag. Maybe your medical assistant can come in and pick some of the pills off the floor. I have them written down on a piece of paper, but when I looked for it today, all I could find was my grocery list. Can you believe the price of strawberries? The organic ones are even more expensive. Do you think I should be eating organic? I've been reading that pesticides can cause cancer, but now that I'm in the doughnut hole, I can't even afford doughnuts, but that's not why I'm here. By the way, your parking's terrible. I drove around for forty minutes before I could find a space, and that reminds me: Can I get a handicapped sticker? I have the form right here. It will only take twenty minutes of your time to fill out, and while you're at it, I'll need a letter to my local YMCA stating that I am fit for water aerobics three times a week. I am sorry to say that your office staff was quite rude when I called yesterday. I realize that it was my third call of the week, but my neighbor told me that cheese might be causing my constipation, and I had just eaten a large hunk of Wisconsin cheddar the day before and hadn't had a bowel movement, and I was worried about an impaction, but that's not the reason I made the appointment.

I saw an advertisement for Cymbalta in my *National Geographic* (I'm a fifty-year subscriber), and I wondered if it could be the eighteenth medicine that might be right for me. I am supposed to tell my health care provider (I think they're referring to you) if I have glaucoma, kidney or liver problems, diabetes, or a seizure disorder. Or maybe I'm bipolar, but shouldn't you already know that if you're my doctor? I need to disclose if I have right upper belly pain, yellow eyes, dark urine, flu-like symptoms, or use alcohol. Is that before or after I start the medicine? It also warns about a peeling rash, skin blisters, sore mouth, dizziness, fainting, sleepiness, headache, weakness, confusion or problems with urine flow. No worry about being pregnant or about to become pregnant or breastfeeding; I'm eighty-seven years old. The ad states that it's indicated for anxiety, depression, fibromyalgia, osteoarthritis, and diabetic neuropathy, and I have this tingling in my elbow after bowling. Is that diabetic neuropathy? Maybe I can't have diabetic neuropathy if I'm not diabetic, but you're the doctor.

I saw Dr. Oz on TV last week. Now there's a compassionate man! You might learn something from him if you watched that show instead of the Golf channel. I don't believe your receptionist when she tells me that you're at the hospital seeing patients. I know you're out playing nine holes, and you pay the woman to lie for you and she's very abrupt on the phone. Did I already mention that? Anyway, during the program, a commercial appeared for Enbrel and you probably know about it because Phil Mickelson, the professional golfer, is in the ad. It stated that it can be used for psoriatic arthritis, and I thought that my sore toe and the rash on my behind might qualify, but I was told to ask you because you're the doctor. I had my daughter download more information on the Internet, I don't own a computer and never will, but I am obligated to inform you if I have any open cuts or sores, diabetes (again), HIV, TB, hepatitis B, heart failure, persistent fever, bruising, paleness, latex allergy, multiple sclerosis, chicken pox, traveled to the Mississippi River Valley (hello! we live there!), or Guillain-Barre. My husband took me to Wilkes-Barre on our honeymoon, is it near there? Then I saw promotions for Boniva, Lipitor, Nexium, and Lunesta, and I have so many things to tell you! I wrote them down in this notebook for you to read. Just cancel your golf game for next Wednesday, and you will have plenty of time to go through it.

OK, enough about myself, I also came to ask about my husband. You see he was ninety years old last May, and he wants to know about Viagra but he is too embarrassed to ask you. He has been impotent for the last ten years but he tells me he'd "like to 'stoke' the fire" again. I read the patient brochure and it states there could be serious vision or hearing problems from taking the medicine, but my husband has been blind and deaf for more than a decade, so I don't think things can get any worse, but you're the doctor. I'll probably need your personal cell phone number to call you in the rare event that he gets an erection that lasts for more than four hours. It says nothing about a feeding tube; can my husband take the medicine if I crush it up and syringe it into his tube with a little Ensure?

I guess I've occupied too much of your time, because since I've been talking you've been staring at your watch. You only made eye contact with me once, and that was when I mentioned Phil Mickelson and a smile came across your face. And by the way, I'll be changing doctors at the end of the year, so this is my last visit. I joined an HMO where there will be no copays and I'll be able to see a nurse practitioner, who I understand is very empathetic. Please have my twenty-five years of records available for me to pick up this afternoon.

Tilly's Pants

I graduated from medical school over forty years ago, and with time the rigors of that endeavor had become a dim memory until I had a chance encounter with my old textbook, *Grants Atlas of Anatomy*, which has been a decades-long competitor of the more famous *Gray's Anatomy* (thanks to a recent television series). One cold January day, I was down in my basement chipping golf balls (the practice variety) into a bookcase that contained my medical books when one of the balls became lodged between the pathology and anatomy tomes. I pulled the old book out and looked inside. It was dog-eared from previous years of usage with the musty smell of an old relic; it probably had not been opened for decades unless a page had inadvertently been exposed as I moved from one place to another. There was a signature inside the front cover, "Property of Jack Margolis," and I realized that this ancient edition had once been my father's. The human body has changed little over the past fifty thousand years except nowadays, DVDs and computer images allow this discipline to be studied with considerably less difficulty.

I never really thought of doing much else in life except becoming a physician. It wasn't that I showed exceptional skills during frog dissections, or that I had performed CPR on an accident victim and miraculously saved his life, or that I spent my summers in college tending to sick orphans in Kenya. Not at all; it was just an unspoken expectation of my parents, and, of course, it's a crowning achievement of any Jewish mother to produce a son who becomes a doctor (my brother is a kidney specialist, so she had two). My father and maternal grandfather were both ophthalmologists. As a gastroenterologist, how many times did I wonder, in the midst of a colonoscopy, why I had not followed in their footsteps? My great-aunt was a physician in the days when very few women were allowed in the profession, and two of my father's sisters were married to doctors. My mother's sister married a rabbi, but that's another story.

Most of the first year was devoted to anatomy, with less time allotted to physiology and biochemistry. On the first day of class, I recall being excited but somewhat apprehensive, and in retrospect, the metaphor "leading a lamb to slaughter" seems pretty apt. I knew fairly quickly that anatomy would be a challenge for me. I have difficulty with spatial cognition, so I was unable to form a mental picture of all the nerves and vessels interwoven amidst the muscles, tendons, and bones. Four medical students shared each cadaver, and we named ours Whitey because of his unsurprisingly pale appearance. We started at the axilla, which is the anatomical term for the armpit, and I learned right then that the medical profession never uses a simple term when an arcane, inscrutable word can be substituted.

Every morning we had a three-hour histology lecture, and we took notes by hand. At the end of the year I had filled several loose-leaf binders, and the subject was so extensive that I told my fellow students before finals that I was trying to plow through one pound per night. Our Hungarian professor tried to make this dry discipline (the Sahara being an ocean in comparison) as entertaining as possible. His legendary response to a former pupil's query about the presence of cilia (fine hair-like structures) on the vaginal cells: "Have you ever seen grass on a race track?" There were other anatomy courses including genetics, embryology, and neuroanatomy, but all I can remember of those subjects was that the brain professor was Dr. Hyde (before he obtained his medical degree, he was Mr. Hyde).

In the afternoon, we entered the dissecting room for a session with Whitey. Our professor, Dr. D, a transplanted Englishman with a countenance akin to a bulldog, reminded me of Winston Churchill in a lab coat. He was a chain smoker, and, of course, in the 1960s you could light one up anytime, anywhere. I recall him coming over to Whitey while we were examining the abdomen, and as he leaned over to show us where the pancreas, was located the ash from his cigarette fell into poor Whitey's abdominal cavity and landed on the dead man's spleen. As the good doctor kept talking, another dropped on his liver. I was not one of Dr. D's favorites as he did not tolerate chatter during his lectures, and I was constantly wise-cracking in the back of the room. One day he heard my prattle, turned on his heel toward me, and announced in a gruff voice that last year there was another medical student with my same attitude, and he was now working at a bank. When my father had attended medical school thirty years previously, the dean had told him that there were four Jews in the class and only two would pass, and in those days, he wasn't kidding. I never told my dad about my run-in with Dr. D, but I worried about failing this subject for the remainder of the academic year.

I generally studied four hours per night and about twelve hours on the weekend. I wore long underwear for several months during the year to keep me warm during the long Manitoba winters, with temperatures often falling to thirty degrees below zero. My dad told me this was "good studying weather," and he was partially correct as there was no enticement on those cold nights to walk to the nearest coffee shop or even drive there with the fear that your car wouldn't start when you got back in the vehicle. On the other hand, grinding over anatomy was never that "good." The amount of information to absorb was at times overwhelming, and I can remember one very anxious evening scrutinizing the bones of the wrist and trying to commit them to memory. The average person is spared throughout his or her life from ever knowing these little buggers, but not the medical student. Even the mnemonic—"Never Lower Tilly's Pants. Mother May Come Home" (Navicular Lunate, Triquetrum, Pisiform, greater Multangular lesser Multangular Capitate, Hamate)—lost its humor after a while.

In high school, I studied Latin for three years with the

thought that this would help me master medical terms; the less gifted kids attended a typing class, because in the pre-computer age this skill was felt to be important for secretaries, not college aspirants. I didn't learn to type until I was fifty, and I'm still quite slow and error prone. The problem with human anatomy is that Latin (and Greek) names are thrown in with everyday words in a haphazard manner. Take for example the segments of the colon. The Latin words *rectum* and *sigmoid* mean straight and "s-shaped" respectively, but the next part is the descending. Descending to where? LaGuardia? And further along there is the ascending colon, not located anywhere near the ass, I might add. The last part of the colon (or the first part depending on which direction you are going) is the *cecum* from the Latin word for "blind," but it's not the only part of the colon that can't see, and the British spelling is *caecum*. Believe me; the Latin I learned has never helped me in my medical career.

By year end we had finally dismembered most of Whitey, but our group hadn't had enough time to dissect the foot. Before the final exam, I took a gamble and ignored this body part hoping that it would not be an essay question even though the tarsal bone mnemonic "Tall California Navy Medical Interns Love Cuties" did pique my interest. The final exam arrived, and no questions on the foot appeared. The results were posted a few days later, and I had passed with the mundane grade of C+. Dr. D had been bluffing, and I didn't need a bank application after all. The exhausting hours of study had paid off, and I was on my way to becoming a doctor. But as I closed the old anatomy text, I shuddered, remembering how difficult that year had been. I was tempted to open my pathology book, a subject that we approached in the second year, but I decided to leave the dust on the cover undisturbed. I had had enough mental angst for one day, and I went back to chipping golf balls.

Things Doctors Never Tell You

Mrs. Tootle, I have no idea why you pass so much gas. If I had a remedy for that, I'd be using it myself, and it might have saved my first marriage.

I'm going to prescribe a more expensive medication, Drug A, rather than the comparable but much cheaper generic Drug X. I met the new rep for Drug A in the break room last week. She is gorgeous, and I couldn't stop looking at her cleavage. I promised her I would write some prescriptions for Drug A.

Mr. Pollock, I know the medical assistant told you to undress, but please put your socks back on. When I entered the room, the bad smell that accosted my nostrils reminded me of the dead mouse that decomposed in our basement last year, but I now realize the odor is coming from your feet.

I'm sorry I had to leave the examining room when my cell phone rang. No, it wasn't the emergency department; it was my wife who just told me that she bought the most expensive dining room table in the store. I told her that somehow I would find a way to pay for it.

I'm going to prescribe the more expensive Drug A rather than the comparable but much cheaper generic Drug X. The pharmaceutical company that manufactures Drug A has hired me as a consultant, and they pay me a one-thousand dollar honorarium with all expenses paid to lovely resorts in the Caribbean where I extol the virtues of this medication to other doctors. I don't see this is a conflict of interest.

I'm sorry I had to leave the examining room when my cell phone rang. No it wasn't the emergency department; it was one of my golf buddies informing me of the tee time for tomorrow afternoon.

Mrs. Green, your husband suffered a serious complication in the operating room. I certainly didn't bring my "A" game today, probably related to a lack of sleep from watching the extra inning ball game last night, but this complication can occur even on my best days.

Mr. Diamond, I'm dismayed to hear that you have declared bankruptcy because of your astronomical medical bills, and I regret that you can't obtain insurance due to preexisting medical conditions, but look on the bright side. You're a great example of "letting the marketplace work." If universal health care was implemented, you wouldn't be broke and would have insurance coverage but you would be extremely disappointed because the government would be involved in making your health care decisions.

I would highly recommend the Acme knee replacement. I am a world authority on the insertion of this prosthesis, and I have written three scientific articles on the stellar results that

I have achieved. Actually the Acme Company wrote those papers, and I just signed my name to them. I am also paid by the company as a consultant, but that's for the hip joint, not the knee joint, so it's not a conflict of interest.

I know I look tired and somewhat disheveled this morning, and it's not because I was performing surgery last night. My wife and I had one doozy of an argument during dinner, and I drank a pint of whiskey before going to bed.

I apologize for being late this afternoon, but it's not what you think. I wasn't delayed in the hospital tending to a critically ill patient; I was in the break room having lunch with a new drug rep who is absolutely gorgeous.

Mrs. Wise, I'm sorry I had to leave when my cell phone rang. My medical assistant has strict instructions to call me after I have been in the examining room with you for more than fifteen minutes. This allows me to take a couple of Alka-Seltzer tablets before I have to listen to any more of your senseless prattle.

I want you to know, Mr. Ryan, that I am absolutely against Obamacare. The physicians at my hospital have already felt the pinch of decreased reimbursements. At one time, there were Maseratis and Mercedes in the doctors' parking lot, but now I see only the cheaper BMW and Lexus models.

To be perfectly honest, Mrs. Bottomley, I lost my concentration while you were describing your voluminous flatulence, and my mind started to wander to the Hindenburg crash of 1937.

The Crooked Cutting Board

I was born in Winnipeg, a cold prairie town in central Canada. In junior high school, I was a nervous skinny kid with above average intelligence, but there was a certain disorganization that seemed to inhibit my achievements. I was fidgety and had trouble focusing on a task, and if I had grown up in the current century, I'm sure I would have been labeled mildly hyperactive. My handwriting was awful, and even though this handicap became a badge of honor when I obtained my medical degree, at that time it seemed to be another impediment in my scholastic progress. I talked incessantly in class and was always trying to get a laugh from the other kids. I was more of a clown than a comedian, but the teachers never found my antics funny. The report cards and teacher conferences repeated a similar theme; I was underachieving. This caused some worry to my parents, particularly my mother who did most of the child rearing, not atypical for a family in the 1960s. I would occasionally get into trouble for acting out in class and once got strapped on the hands by my seventh-grade science teacher (corporal punishment was still acceptable in those days) for making unsolicited wisecracks in the classroom when we were dissecting frogs. I tearfully told the story to my mother when I came home from school. She immediately became incensed and paid a visit to Mr. G, the science teacher, the next morning, and as she later told me, she "wiped the floor with him." I'm sure that the punishment was less traumatic to me than to Mr. G when he had to face the wrath of my mother. I know these screw-ups caused her some disappointment, but she always maintained a rosy optimism in regard to my talents.

In 1959, part of the eight-grade curriculum was industrial arts. The woodworking program involved making a cutting board for our mothers (fathers weren't cooking in those days). I recently Googled my old school, and to my amazement, the curriculum for the novice woodworker still includes the "cutting board" over fifty years later, only now the instructions are available on the Internet. I remember being filled with optimism as I started the project. We had to cut a piece of wood to specifications using a back saw, and then file the top corners to gently round them. It was then sanded, and a hole was drilled near the top so it could be hung on a hook. We put a stain on the board and presented it to the teacher for grading. My project received a C, only due to the kindness of the shop teacher. The rounded corners at the upper border were asymmetric, and the hole for hanging was off-center. Although in some circles this might have been passed off as a piece of cubism art, in the eighth grade it was just an example of sloppy work done by an unfocused child. My mother received it cheerfully and told me that the last Jewish carpenter was Joseph, so I needn't worry about making it a career. She immediately began to use it to cut vegetables and hung it in a prominent place above the stove.

There was also some anxiety on her part in regard to my weight. I was mostly a skeleton with an epidermis. Growing up in Canada, we did not have a school cafeteria, so we brought our lunch from home. Most of the mothers included a sandwich, an apple, and a few sweets; not my mother. She would make me a quintuple-decker masterpiece of French bread stuffed with tuna fish, sardines, egg salad, chicken, pickles, olives, cream cheese, and an assortment of vegetables. This was accompanied by freshly baked chocolate chip or oatmeal cookies. The other kids really liked my lunches, and I gave most of them away each day. Her dinners were sumptuous; I particularly remember her stewed brisket and the meat loaf with an egg in the center. Our birthdays fell on the same day. She told me every year that I was the best birthday present that she had ever received. She annually produced a delicious birthday cake with a dark chocolate filling and a lighter chocolate icing, probably 1500 calories per slice. She had one blind spot involving my eating, and that centered on calf liver. At that time, it was an important part of every child's diet. I hated liver, particularly when it was fried and combined with onions. I had to sit at the dinner table until I finished every morsel. At one bite per fifteen minutes, I sat there for a long time.

As I continued with my adolescence, I slowly outgrew

my hyperactivity and became a fairly good student, although my terrible handwriting was still a setback. My mother went back to school and completed a master's degree in psychology. I entered the local university at the same time, and we attended together. I remember helping her with her statistics class. Her school work never prevented her from continuing to produce fabulous dinners on a regular basis. I did much better scholastically in college than high school and was accepted to medical school. She knitted a thick woolen sweater that I wore on those cold wintery evenings when I was studying my anatomy and physiology texts.

Time passed. I moved to St Louis and became extremely busy with my medical practice, wife, and two children. My parents retired to California. I talked with my mother frequently on the telephone, and I saw her about once a year, but I stopped visiting her on our birthday. My life came crashing down with my divorce when I was in my mid-forties. My mother, as usual, was there as my support, and she and my dad came to St. Louis and helped me set up my apartment. She gave me some of her great recipes, and I began cooking for myself. I resumed the regular birthday reunions and she continued to bake the chocolate cake, and now I had the appetite to really enjoy it.

Our last birthday dinner took place when she was 79 and I was 52. She was still a great cook but I noticed that she had become a little forgetful; unfortunately it was the first ravages of Alzheimer's disease. We went to her favorite grocery store, the Pavilion in Rancho Mirage, California, to buy food for the meal. I noticed that she was moving through the store much more slowly than I had remembered, and it took us a long time to make our purchases. When we got home, I volunteered to make the salad. I opened the pantry to get some utensils, and then I saw it. The wood was frayed and discolored, but there was no mistaking the cockeyed sides and the eccentric hole. I couldn't believe that she had kept that poor piece of workmanship all those years. I remarked, "you surely don't use it anymore," and she replied, "I don't use it for all the vegetables, only the onions." With that, she gave me a couple from the grocery bag, and I began to chop them on my old crooked cutting board. I suddenly started to cry, but the tears weren't from the onions. They were from my heart.

Favey

When I was eight years old my mother bought me three flannel shirts. They were yellow, green, and red and had black lines running through, so as to form squares on top of the background colors. On the first day that I put on the yellow shirt, I scored a goal in the soccer game that was held daily at recess. In my boyish mind, I attributed that good fortune to the new shirt I was wearing, and I gave it the name Favey, short for favorite. The following day I put on the green shirt, and I was sent to the principal's office for misbehaving in class. After that, I came to believe that some misadventure might befall me when I was wearing that shirt, as opposed to my invincibility when I was wearing Favey. Even my mother started to call the shirt Favey, and she knew that if I had a test or a presentation, she better have the yellow shirt clean and ready to wear. All the shirts in the closet soon acquired an anthropomorphic quality. Favey was the top gun, but I was careful to wear all the other shirts in rotation so as not to hurt their feelings. I never had the same sentiments about pants or underwear, only the shirts.

This seemed like a satisfactory arrangement until I adopted an imaginary friend named Joe Malone. I'm not sure why a Jewish kid had an ethereal companion with an Irish name, but so be it. Joe came to me when I was alone, in the evening and early morning. In the mid 1950s, there was no Nintendo or Xbox to amuse oneself, and there were only a few children's shows on TV. Joe was my opponent in the simulated hockey game that I played with my right and left hands with one die that I borrowed from my Monopoly set. The opposing baseboards in our upstairs hallway served as goals, and I spent countless hours playing with Joe. The trouble began when Joe developed a liking for the red shirt, and a rivalry ensued between Joe and Favey. One morning when I went to the closet, I forgot which shirt was to be worn that day, so I selected the red one after consulting with Joe. I could see that Favey was seething, but what could I do? Joe had his heart set on the red shirt. I went off to school, and of course, Joe stayed home. During recess we had our usual rough-and-tumble soccer game and unfortunately the shirt was badly ripped. When I returned home my mother examined it, declared it a total loss, and put it in the rag pile. Joe appeared and was obviously despondent by the loss of his friend. Favey wore a smug look as if to say that he knew all along that it was a mistake to pick the red shirt.

The next morning when I awoke, I knew that a difficult decision awaited me. There was an arithmetic test that day involving fractions, and arithmetic always made me nervous. I needed the confidence of Favey, but I knew that Joe was still mourning the red shirt and would be angry if I chose his adversary when he was in such a vulnerable state. The only clean shirts available were the green one and Favey. At first, I was going to cop out with an eenie, meenie, miney, moe pick, but then I had a change of heart. I grabbed the green shirt, put it on, and began fastening the buttons. I could sense the icy hostility of Favey perched on his hanger, and suddenly I developed acute pretest anxiety. Not only was I not wearing my lucky shirt, but even worse, I had on the blighted green one. When I arrived in class, I slumped down into my desk and waited for the test to begin. The teacher handed out the paper and I perused the questions. I started to concentrate and soon became engrossed in the mental effort. To my surprise, I did not have any trouble solving the equations and scored a 90% on the test. My only misstep was the pie problem. If you cut a pie in half and then divide each half into thirds and you eat one half of one of the thirds, how much of that pie have you eaten? I had put down one-sixth when the answer was one-twelfth. I thought to myself, maybe I would have obtained the right answer if Favey had been with me, but it was also possible that if I had read the question more carefully, I would have arrived at the correct result whether Favey was present or not. I came home from school and proudly showed my mother the exam paper. I headed up to my room where Joe was waiting to offer congratulations. Favey looked glum and sulked for the rest of the evening.

After that experience, I began to realize that my garment selection wasn't all that important. Favey was still number one, but my successes or failures might not depend on the shirt on my back. Several months later, I spilled some ink on Favey while filling my cartridge pen (that's what we used in the 1950s). My mother tried to remove the stain, but the shirt was irretrievably damaged, and anyway, it was getting a little snug on me. The last time I saw Favey, he was being used to polish the chrome on our 1954 Oldsmobile.

A few years ago, when I was in my late fifties, I bought a short-sleeved shirt from the Lands' End catalogue. This was a yellow, green, and red-checked shirt. When I opened the box, the recollection of Favey swept over me. I retold the story to my wife. She gave me a perplexed look and turned down one corner of her mouth. She told me the shirt was "nice," but I could see that she didn't particularly like it. I thought about Joe Malone and tried to contact him, but I found out from his imaginary son that he had gone to the imaginary grave many decades ago. After wearing Favey II for a while, I discovered that I didn't like the color combination nor the feel of it on my body (it was made of a synthetic blend of cotton and polyester). It's currently for sale at the Goodwill store near our house. Now as I lurch toward the end of my life, I only have a dim memory of Favey, Joe, and the third grade. Even my beloved mother passed away several years ago. Yet I will never forget the joy that I once had when I buttoned that yellow flannel shirt, marched downstairs, and thought I could conquer the world.

Mythology and Colonoscopy

Asclepius, the great physician-god, had spent eons observing the medical advances of civilization, but he had become depressed. Once, he had been the most celebrated doctor in the classical world; Greeks and their contemporaries came from all over to subject themselves to his healing powers. But sadly, he had not treated a patient for over 2500 years.

He was the son of Apollo and Coronis, but his mother was killed at his birth when Apollo discovered that she had been unfaithful. Asclepius was raised by a centaur—half man and half horse—named Chiron who taught him how to heal wounds, quell fevers, and treat plagues using salves, potions, and incantations. He also acquired the power to raise the dead. One day, after killing a serpent that had wrapped around his staff, another snake appeared with a special herb in his mouth and restored the first snake to life. After that, Asclepius used this substance to resurrect the deceased, particularly a man named Hippolytus, who had been killed by his stepmother. These acts angered Zeus, the supreme god, for he believed that if humans could return to living, it would destroy the natural cycle of man's time on earth. He hurled one of his legendary thunderbolts at the august physician, catapulted him into the heavens, and made him a god. After his death, temples with herpetariums were built in his honor and the populace attended these holy sanctuaries to affect cures for their ailments, but that had been ages ago. In modern times, his staff with the entwined serpent had remained renowned, and physician societies and medical schools still used that image on their letterheads and in their yearbooks, but most contemporary practitioners had scant knowledge of this eminent healer's accomplishments.

In his celestial residence, Asclepius watched superstar clinicians perform their art: Hippocrates, Aristotle, Galen, and even Benjamin Rush and William Osler in the United States. He observed Harvey's studies of blood circulation, Jenner's development of the small pox vaccine, Fleming's discovery of penicillin, and Banting's formulation of insulin. All this time, Asclepius was itching to get back to practicing medicine. One afternoon, he was browsing the ethernet when he came across an article about a black, snake-like object with a powerful lighted eye that traveled through the body on the direction of a physician. As Asclepius looked down at his serpent encircling his walking stick, he saw a striking resemblance between his old friend and the mechanical instrument. He read further about this machine and learned that it was called a colonoscope.

Asclepius went to the quarterly conclave of the gods on

Mt. Olympus and begged their permission to reincarnate and employ this snake-like tool. Zeus was reluctant to give his approval and told him that working as a doctor in modern society would be completely different from his experience in classical Greece, but Hermes and Mars came to his defense after mentioning the popular perfume and candy bars that respectively bore their names. Zeus felt somewhat guilty about zapping the erstwhile healer in the peak of his prime, so he relented and gave permission for Asclepius to become one of the living again.

Max Sokolov came from a long line of prominent physicians. His father and grandfather, as well as several uncles, were doctors, and his brother Ben was an academic nephrologist with a worldwide reputation. Sokolov completed his gastroenterology training in one of the top centers in the country but had chosen to return to his home town where both he and his wife had spent their childhood. He hammered up his shingle in a thriving community just outside of the city limits; however, in the thirty years that Sokolov had been in practice, the area had fallen on hard times with the flight of Caucasians to the distant exurbs. Now his practice consisted of the elderly, minorities, and the poor. Nevertheless, he was extremely busy and had developed a well-earned reputation for compassion and competence. He came home at nights exhausted with little time for his wife, children, or grandchildren and his golf game suffered from lack of playing time. At last, he decided that he needed to find an associate with the thought that he would phase out over a period of years and then retire.

He placed ads in all the medical journals and attended the national convention of gastroenterologists, seeking a subordinate to join him. He even hired a head hunter. A few applicants showed interest, but when they saw his rundown office and his patient clientele, they were unimpressed and Sokolov never heard from them again. He was about ready to give up and contemplated closing the operation entirely, when he received a call from the recruiter. He was told that a gentleman from Greece would be coming for an interview.

When the fellow arrived for his appointment, Sokolov was taken aback by his appearance. He had the swarthy complexion of a man from the Mediterranean, he spoke with a Greek accent, and there was a faint smell of body odor. He was almost bald, with a straggly grey beard, an aquiline nose, and tufts of hair extruding from his rather large ears. The man wore open-toed sandals and a faded sport jacket with leather patches on his elbows, a style that was popular in the 1970s, and Sokolov could have sworn that he was wearing a toga. He leaned on a cane with a carving on the top in the image on an animal, possibly a snake, and he carried a strange satchel with him that Sokolov found out later was a goat's bladder. They shook hands, and Sokolov asked him his name. "In this country I go by Dr. A. S. Clepius, but just call me Cleppy." Sokolov inquired about his training. "I worked with Chiron in Greece and received most of my gastroenterology experience on Mt Olympus." Sokolov had no knowledge of Greek teaching programs, but in the U.S., Chiron was a biotechnology company and Olympus was the largest manufacturer of colonoscopes. Cleppy added, "I have been in the United States for three months to learn English, and I was able to obtain a temporary medical license until my references arrive, which might take some time as they have been archived for many years." Sokolov showed the applicant around. He seemed intrigued with the equipment, particularly the scopes. Although the gastroenterologist thought Dr. Clepius rather strange, he was friendly and polite, and thus Sokolov was willing to overlook his obscure training and bizarre persona. Plus he was desperate. The next day, after discussing the candidate with his wife, he offered the man a job, with the possibility of a partnership. To the doctor's astonishment, the Hellene immediately accepted.

Three weeks later Cleppy started his new employment. He was wearing the same peculiar outfit. Sokolov advised him to take off the sport jacket, and he gave him an oversized lab coat to cover most of the toga, along with a stick of deodorant. There were three patients in the holding area awaiting colonoscopy, and Sokolov was on his way to the hospital, so he turned them over to the Greek. Dr. Clepius worked slowly on the first case, and the nurse assisting him noticed that he was unfamiliar with the equipment. As he started up the colon, he kept banging against the walls and was making little progress. The nurse was about to place a call to Sokolov to help the inept operator, when suddenly Cleppy began to hum a strange tune, almost like a hymn, and immediately the scope started to move and eventually reached the *cecum* (the end of the colon or the beginning depending on the direction you're heading). The following two examinations proceeded in the same manner, but it had taken him the whole morning to complete just three procedures where Sokolov normally did ten or twelve.

That afternoon, Cleppy saw a few patients in the clinic. The first patient, Bertha Tootle, was diagnosed with irritable bowel syndrome years ago. Sokolov had not been able to help the woman's bloating and flatulence but was sympathetic, so she kept coming back year after year with the same complaints. After listening to her recite those ailments, Cleppy pulled out some greenery from his sack without performing a physical exam or ordering any lab tests. "This is thapsian, a plant that I used in Greece for just such a problem. Make some tea from these leaves, and your symptoms will improve. Hippocrates used this remedy and he was quite successful." Mrs. Tootle left the office pleased that her new physician had at least a fresh approach—instead of the pessimistic Sokolov—when it came to her condition. The next patients included Mr. Orville Lush with alcoholic cirrhosis, Ms. Lexy Forsythe complaining of a belly ache, and young Sam Tonopolsky with acid reflux. Cleppy went through the same routine; he reached into his bag for an herb or an ointment and even sang a song for the kid with heartburn.

A few problems did crop up. Cleppy told the patients that they could pay whatever they determined was appropriate. If they had a few pieces of gold, a chicken or some vegetables, it was fine with him. Of course none of these patients had any of these objects in their possession, so they ended up paying nothing. He didn't take any notes on the computer during these visits, but wrote down a few words in Greek on a scrap of paper. When Sokolov returned from the hospital, he was notified by his employees about the Hellene's strange colonoscopic technique as well as his unorthodox performance with the clinic patients. He brought Cleppy into his office and emphasized the need to fill out the billing forms so that insurance would reimburse the practice, and stressed that barter was not an acceptable method of payment. He again explained the computer program, underscoring the need for documentation and the consequences of their absence if there was ever a malpractice suit. The Greek seemed puzzled by these criticisms and he didn't comprehend the words "insurance" and "malpractice suit." He told Sokolov that he believed he had done a good job, and was particularly gratified that he could work with a snake again, albeit a mechanical one. Sokolov was beginning to realize that hiring Dr. Clepius might have been a mistake, and his curious reptile talk was disquieting to say the least.

A month went by, but Cleppy's production was still below par, and Sokolov was disheartened at the sluggish progress. He signed the Greek's first paycheck and handed it over to him. Cleppy was dismayed by the paltry sum. Although the gross pay was the amount that he had agreed to, after deductions there was only sixty-five percent remaining. Sokolov patiently explained the withholding of Social Security, Medicare, and income taxes, and mentioned that after paying the secretary and nurse's salary, as well as the hefty malpractice bill, he was actually losing money on his new assistant. Cleppy did not grasp most of this elucidation, but he yearned for the days when he could collect some virgin olive oil or goat cheese for his services, and he began to recognize that a manufactured scope could never replace his faithful serpent.

The next morning, Mrs. Tootle returned to the office with a huge smile on her face. Her flatus had markedly diminished with the medicine given to her by the toga-clad physician. Similarly, Lush's jaundice had receded, Ms. Forsythe's pain had abated, and little Tonopolsky no longer had indigestion. The office staff was impressed with Cleppy's treatment, and word got back to Sokolov who was startled that the eccentric practitioner had actually had some success.

Sokolov had not taken any time off for three years, and his wife had suggested an Italian cruise for their thirty-fifth wedding anniversary. Although he was hesitant to leave the practice to Dr. Clepius, he did not want to disappoint his spouse, so they departed for a two-week vacation in Europe. The following day, Selma Whiteside arrived for an office visit referred by her primary physician, Dr. Phil Morris. She had expected to find Sokolov, but instead Cleppy entered the exam room and explained that the senior physician was on vacation. Selma was in her late seventies but acted much younger. She inquired as to Cleppy's heritage, and when he replied that he was Greek, they had a lively discussion about her trip to Corfu many years ago. Cleppy immediately sensed a connection with this woman, and her rather unruly grey hair reminded him of the godlike Medusa who had once helped him with his medical studies. Selma mentioned that she had developed extreme fatigue and had passed some blood from her rectum. Dr. Morris had drawn lab work, which revealed that she was anemic. Dr. Clepius recommended a colonoscopy when Sokolov returned, but she was so taken with the Greek that she requested that he perform the procedure, so Cleppy agreed.

The colonoscopy was done a few days later. Cleppy was becoming familiar with the workings of the instrument and managed to reach the cecum in forty minutes, which was an improvement for him. He was congratulating himself on his success when he saw a reddish protuberance in that area. This resembled a large piece of beefsteak with a central depression. When the scope contacted the tumor, the lesion bled easily, and there was no doubt that this was the source of her symptoms; moreover, it had the obvious appearance of colon cancer. He took some biopsies, which came back positive. Selma underwent an operation, and unfortunately the news was dire. The malignancy had spread into the liver and throughout the abdominal cavity. The surgeon was unable to remove the primary tumor from the colon, so he sewed her back up and relayed the tragic news to Dr. Morris and her family. Cleppy visited her frequently while she recuperated. Although she kept a cheerful exterior, Selma knew that the prognosis was dismal, but she continued to chat with Cleppy about his country of origin and displayed a thorough knowledge of Greek mythology as well. She asked about his family and his medical training. She was about the only person who had taken any interest in him since he had entered the twenty-first century. Selma was eventually discharged and was referred to an oncologist for some dubious chemotherapy.

When Sokolov returned, the office was in disarray. Cleppy had continued his haphazard methods, and his slow pace had left many irate patients fuming in the waiting room, as they had fasted for their colonoscopies, which were three hours behind schedule. He decided that his new associate had to go. Cleppy, for his part, was feeling the extreme pressure of medical practice: the volume of patients, the constant telephone calls, the mountains of paper work, and the pervasive threat of lawsuits. He now understood that today's medicine was much more difficult in reality than when observed from the constellations. Sokolov brought the Greek into the office and announced the bad news. Cleppy was to be terminated in two weeks. The look of resignation on his countenance indicated that he was not surprised.

That night Cleppy received a call from the emergency room. Mrs. Whiteside had returned and was hemorrhaging from the colon. He hung up the phone, buttoned up his badly wrinkled lab coat, and took the long walk to the hospital (he had never learned to drive). Selma looked pale and her breathing was labored, but she was still alert and seemed pleased to see him. It was obvious that the tumor, which had not been extirpated, had started to bleed, and Cleppy knew that another colonoscopy would be futile. The ER physician discussed her situation with Dr. Morris, and they agreed to admit Selma to the hospital for end-of-life care. Dr. Clepius felt helpless, like physicians from time immemorial, but there was nothing more he could do—or was there? He ran back to his apartment, rummaged through the goat bladder, and found the potion that he had used on Hippolytus a few millennia ago. The heck with Zeus; he was on his way back to the heavens anyway, and Zeus hadn't fired a thunderbolt in over two thousand years. He returned to the hospital and gave the dying woman the concoction in a small paper cup at the bedside.

The following morning, the bleeding had abated, and Selma was her usual chipper self. Morris thought that this was probably related to a blood transfusion that had been administered the night before. She was released from the hospital and never bled again. A CT scan performed several weeks later showed that the tumors had shrunk dramatically, and the oncologist congratulated himself on the excellence of his treatment.

Asclepius returned to the starry sky and resumed his ethereal existence. At the next deity's meeting, he vented his frustrations with practicing medicine in the twenty-first century, and related his encounter with Selma Whiteside. After he finished, he slumped on his staff, preparing for an angry retort from Zeus, but the all-powerful just shrugged his shoulders and wore a wry smile as if to say, "I told you so."

Sleepless in Cleveland

I decided in my third year of medical school to obtain an internal medicine internship and applied to several U.S. hospitals. My father had been an ophthalmology resident in Chicago and was insistent that I continue my training south of the Canadian border, so I took his advice and moved to Cleveland in 1971. This was during the Vietnam War, but being a Canadian, I had no fear of being drafted, unlike many of my fellow interns who ultimately served in that conflict.

The chief of neurology at the hospital I chose had been a classmate of my father's, and I thought that he would take me under his wing, but regrettably this special nurturing never materialized. On my first week, I passed him in the hallway, and after a brief hello, he told me that we would talk some more, but he needed to get home to put a prime rib in the oven. Gee, this renowned professor cooking a roast didn't exactly fit with my idea of the great physician and teacher. I never found out whether he liked his beef well-done or rare, because he never invited me to dinner, ever. He did take me to one football game of the Cleveland Browns before they moved to Baltimore and became the Ravens and then restarted again as the Browns. So in Cleveland I was pretty much on my own, but it was there that I learned to be a doctor, the hard way.

Cleveland in the 1970s was not Paris, London, or even Cincinnati. The first year I was there, the Cuyahoga River caught fire, and the pollution from the steel mills and chemical factories was so strong it made my eyes water. The acrid smell in the air was a sensation that my nostrils had never experienced in Canada. I shared living space with a junior resident, and we hardly saw each other as most nights at least one of us was on call at the hospital. My diet was poor in those years, mostly carryout fast food, and the apartment was littered with old pizza boxes and McDonald's wrappers. The dwelling was never cleaned properly, and the kitchen floor was covered with a greasy film that stuck to the bottom of your soles if you walked barefoot. We occasionally had some young ladies over for the evening, and believe me, they needed to be brave or desperate to spend any time at that place.

On the first day, I remember nervously putting on my starched white jacket and pants, thinking that I might do better as an ice cream vendor than a doctor. Most of the patients that we treated were indigent, often homeless, and lacked health insurance. They were usually admitted via the emergency room and often arrived at the hospital wards from ten p.m. to three a.m. The intern taking call would therefore be awake most of the night. At about five a.m., if he was lucky, he could get a short catnap before waking for rounds at seven. We took call every third night for the entire year. This was the ultimate in sleep deprivation. After my short siesta, I could function for about three or four hours, but after that my mind would be in a fog until I went to bed the next evening; occasionally I would nod off at the wheel while driving home from the hospital. The day after call, the severely fatigued intern was still expected to care for the very sick individuals in the hospital as well as attend an afternoon clinic with outpatients. I can recall introducing myself to a polite elderly lady with diabetes and hypertension and then promptly dozing off as she listed her complaints. I woke up and looked at my watch, and about fifteen minutes had gone by. I apologized and then continued on with my history. I don't recollect the woman's reaction, but she had little choice but to return to our free clinic for her next appointment. Another time, one of my fellow interns and I were on rounds with the attending physician when my friend, who had been on duty that night, presented his patient and then promptly fell into a deep slumber. The doctor turned away from him and directed his remarks to me as if nothing had occurred, while my colleague made quiet but audible snoring sounds, his head intermittently undergoing spastic flexion on his chest akin to a bobblehead doll.

I had a middle-class upbringing and had never encountered the destitute human beings that I treated at that institution. In my first week on the job, an alcoholic was admitted to me with a severely damaged liver. He informed me that he was drinking two bottles of Mad Dog 20/20 per day. I had never heard of this beverage until my resident explained to me that Mad Dog stood for Mogen David, the liquid of choice for some inebriates. I had thought this wine was reserved solely for the Passover Seder. The following day, the patient went into alcohol withdrawal with hallucinations and agitation. The only effective therapy in those days was to place him in leather restraints and administer sedation rectally, while hoping to keep an intravenous line in place. There was no intensive care unit, and patients were placed on ventilators in a standard hospital room. On my first rotation, a breathing tube kinked during the night, and when I made rounds the following day, the unfortunate person had been dead for several hours. One morning, I awoke to the sound of the classical guitar and saw one of the other interns playing the instrument at the nurses' station. He had neglected all of his patients that night, and it was obvious that he had suffered a psychotic break. We never saw him again. At first I was shocked by these happenings, but somewhat like a combat veteran, I eventually accepted it as a way of life with a surreal aura compounded by the miasma of insomnia.

We had scant ancillary support. In addition to taking care of very ill people, the intern's duties were to draw blood, stamp requisitions, and even wheel patients to the X-ray department in the evening when the transporters had gone home—so called scut work. The professors came by only a few times per week, leaving the interns and residents on their own much of the day and night. Several years ago Medicare mandated that there be a daily notation by an attending physician, but that was long after I had completed my medical training.

Occasionally, we needed to consult the chief surgical resident in the wee hours of the morning, and we prepared to have our butts chewed out no matter the circumstance. If the patient needed surgery, he ranted that we should have called him in earlier; if he determined that the person did not need his services, he reamed us out for waking him up.

I wasn't particularly enamored with the chief of Internal Medicine, who was my ultimate boss. Dr. R was a gruff individual with a lined, weather-beaten face and was well past his prime. He smoked one unfiltered Pall Mall after another and drank several cups of strong black coffee during the daily resident's report. I was somewhat of a rebel and was disparaging of the old man for making us perform the scut work. I never criticized him to his face, but I'm sure that my body language in his presence indicated disapproval. When I started my final year, he hosted a weekend for the senior residents at his beach cottage on Lake Michigan, but I found an excuse not to attend.

I struggled through my internship and somehow managed to survive. The second year as a junior resident was less exhausting as we rotated through subspecialties such as gastroenterology and cardiology, but in the third year we were placed back on the wards as senior residents. My first rotation that year was Male Medicine (the floors were segregated by sex), and I had three interns working under me. One day, our group had had a particularly bad day. There had been several admissions to our service, and there were no beds available. Today, those patients are kept in the emergency room or holding areas until they can be transferred to the hospital floors, but at that time, these poor souls were brought to the ward and placed in the hallway. On this particular night, four or five of these sick men were lying on stretchers without a room. We couldn't examine them or even obtain vital signs. At that juncture, my anger rose, probably aggravated by lack of sleep, and I made a very foolish decision. At about six a.m. we wheeled a confused man with pneumonia over to the hospital president's office and left him in the hallway in front of his door. Of course, the executive totally blew his stack when he arrived that morning and encountered the poor fellow blocking the entrance to his office. A few hours later I was called on the carpet by Dr. R who bawled me out for being irresponsible and advised me that there would be a conference of the top brass to decide my fate. I went home that evening fearing that I would be fired and my medical career would be in jeopardy. How could I have done such a stupid thing? I had risked an individual's life to prove a point, even though my argument had some merit. I had never got along very well with Dr. R, and now I wished that I had been more discreet in my feelings as he considered my termination. A few days later, I had another meeting with him, and to my relief he told me they were going to let me keep my job, but I was on probation. Fortunately, I managed to finish the year without further adverse events.

That dreadful incident taught me never to subordinate a patient's well-being to my own personal issues, and I remembered that lesson for all of the thirty-six years of my medical practice. I learned that there are ways to disagree with your superiors without alienating them, and that chronic complainers are never popular in the workplace.

I've always looked upon that episode as a turning point in my life. It was the watershed moment when my parents' influence waned, and I was on my own to fend my way through the world. I guess the harsh crucible of hopelessly sick patients, sleepless nights, tongue lashings by my superiors, and impossible workloads had forged the doctor inside of me. I packed up my car and headed west on Highway 70. The boy who had arrived with a medical diploma with the ink hardly dry was left behind and replaced by a young man and a physician. I was on my way to St. Louis to become a gastroenterologist and master the technique of colonoscopy. I was to learn about the "butt light" in the city of the "Bud Light."

The Ox that Ate Lox

There once was an ox, who loved to eat lox,
But noshing on lox caused a pox on his hocks.
The pox on his hocks so tormented the ox,
That he consulted three docs to find a cure for his pox.
He was prescribed pills in a box for the pox on his hocks,
But the pox on his hocks, after eating the lox,
Didn't get well from the pills in the box,
So he went to a fox for the pox on his hocks.
He was told by the fox, that it wasn't a pox,
Just knocks to his hocks from walks over rocks,
And he was given some socks to cushion the shocks.
The ox resumed his craving for lox,
And he thanked the fox for healing his hocks.
Sometimes a fox knows more than three docs.

The First Seven Days of My Diet

DAY ONE: I wake up at five a.m and rush downstairs for thirty minutes on my treadmill before going to work. My breakfast consists of a bowl of Cheerios with skim milk and fresh blackberries bought the day before at the local Piggly Wiggly. I make a lunch of low-calorie bread with a dab of plain hummus, an apple, and an orange, with an eco-friendly reusable container for water. As soon as I reach the office, I am reminded that one of the secretaries is retiring and there is a special lunch scheduled. I will look like a sap if I show up with my brown bag, so I put my healthy fare in the refrigerator and eat the catered meal. It's Mexican food, and while talking to the staff, I munch on a few too many salsa chips and the guacamole dip is delicious—a few enchiladas and a burrito, hey I have to be sociable—but I did drink a diet Coke. Now how could I refuse some chocolate retirement cake? I'm feeling somewhat guilty, but that evening I enjoy a lovely dinner of chicken breast with broccoli florets. Regrettably, our little Girl Scout neighbor delivers the cookies that very evening, and I nibble on some Thin Mints while chatting with her father.

DAY TWO: I was up most of the night with heartburn and slept late; it could have been those additional cookies before bed or maybe the glass of wine. No time to work out or have breakfast at home. The McDonalds is very close to the office, and the drive-in is convenient. I scan the menu in my car for a reduced-calorie meal, but there is hardly any line behind me, and the next thing I know I'm ordering, so I select my usual Bacon Egg and Cheese Bagel. I still have my healthy lunch, but as luck would have it, the perky drug rep is there today and she has brought in pizza for the entire staff. It's the deep dish variety, my very favorite.

As we discuss the latest news about her pharmaceuticals, I proceed to eat three slices along with some chocolate chip cookies. I have a long day and arrive home to find out that my wife had car trouble and couldn't get to the grocery, so couldn't we just go out tonight? By the time we're seated at the restaurant, I'm extremely hungry, and the server brings six hot rolls with butter while we are perusing the menu, and suddenly the basket is empty. I order the chicken sandwich, which seems quite innocuous calorie-wise, but I fail to appreciate that it comes with a load of French fries.

DAY THREE: I'm exhausted from yesterday's demanding schedule. I grab a donut as I leave the house. At lunch, I look for Monday's meal, but the staff tells me that they cleaned out the refrigerator yesterday and must have thrown it out. It's already two in the afternoon and all I can find is leftover pizza, but it tastes even better than the day before. My evening meal is a success until I'm ambushed later in the evening by the remainder of the Thin Mints.

DAY FOUR: This is it. No more screw-ups. I begin exercising, but after five minutes a call comes in from the hospital and I need to be there right away. I look for my Cheerios, but all I see is a box of Fruit Loops. Too late to make a lunch, but I'll eat a salad at the hospital. When I arrive at the doctor's lounge, the lettuce looks wilted and the salad dressing is Thousand Island; I might as well eat the main course, which consists of roast beef and mashed potatoes with heavy gravy. Now why would they serve that to doctors?

DAY FIVE: I start on the treadmill, but soon I feel a pain in my groin. I hope it's not arthritis in my hip. Today there is no cereal at all in the pantry, so I head for the McDonald's again but resolve not to eat any lunch, and I will still come out all right for the day. But late in the afternoon I become hypoglycemic, and there are still five people in the waiting room. I find the chocolate cake from the retirement party; it's a bit stale but I'll just have a small piece. OK, two pieces, and one of the nurses brought in some homemade brownies. I counsel the last patient on a weight-reducing diet. When I finally get home, I'm informed that we are dining at a French restaurant with Dr. Fressen and his wife. He is my best referring physician. Now I dare you to order a low-calorie meal at an upscale French restaurant!

DAY SIX: I'm off today. I attend my yoga class, but then the whole group congregates for bagels and cream cheese. I traipse to the mall with my wife to buy a new food processor; I plan to make some reduced-calorie soups. We stop for lunch, and I'm determined to eat healthy. I order the "Thai Crunch Salad" and congratulate myself on my willpower, but afterwards, when I check the nutritional content online, I find it's 1200 calories. My grandson comes for dinner, and hotdogs are his favorite food.

DAY SEVEN: In the morning the little kid is still there, and he loves to go to Denny's for breakfast. He keeps repeating "pancakes, pancakes" in this pathetic little voice. How can I turn him down? At the Denny's, I show him off to the other customers while we wait for our meal, but when the food arrives, I find out he isn't as hungry as he had thought, and I end up eating most of his pancakes as well as my own.

At home, I begin to prepare my soup. I'm just learning to cook. The recipe calls for some peppers. I buy some small peppers and throw three or four into the broth. A few hours later I sample my masterpiece, but the liquid is so hot it feels as though I have a second-degree burn on my tongue. I tell my wife that the peppers were Habaneros, and she tells me to throw the entire concoction down the drain, and we eat out at the local burger joint.

Early the next day, I have my first weigh-in since the start of my diet. To my shock I have gained another two pounds!

All right, I had a few lapses. I chug down to the basement stairs for thirty minutes on the treadmill, and then eat a low calorie breakfast of Cheerios, skim milk, and blackberries.

Dr. Kugelman's Obsession

Norman Kugelman was a decent man. He was a highly successful gastroenterologist but nevertheless had compassion for the less fortunate, and would treat patients for free if they lacked health insurance. He was available to his patients seven days a week and rarely took a vacation. Kugelman attended religious services religiously, and was a former president of his synagogue. His lifestyle was comfortable, and his investments were profitable so that he had enough money to retire early if he so desired. A generous fellow, he gave a considerable portion of his salary to several charities and volunteered to build a house with Habitat for Humanity, even though his skill as a carpenter, like that of most Jewish men, was minimal.

He had met his wife Selma at college. At the time, she had been mildly attractive, but the years had taken their toll, and she had gained a considerable amount of weight in the wrong places since he had stolen her away from Howard Fishman at the fraternity Hanukah party. She had quit college to rear their two boys and had never obtained her degree. With time, Selma became rather dissatisfied with her lack of professional skills, and I believe she subconsciously blamed Norman, whose impregnation had resulted in a hasty wedding. She constantly nitpicked at him about little things such as leaving his dirty underwear in the middle of the bedroom floor, forgetting to take out the garbage on the appropriate day, and, of course, there were issues with the toilet seat, particularly at night. Norman was resigned to her complaining, and being the upright man that he was, he tolerated her occasional despondency. He had never been unfaithful.

Norman's life would have been quite satisfying if not for his constant craving for pork which, of course, was against Jewish dietary laws. Unfortunately, Norman had a legacy of Jewish pork eating. His grandfather, who had emigrated from Russia, found a job in a meat-packing plant while scraping together enough money to open his own butcher shop. To the surprise of his relatives, he started selling non-kosher meat to gentiles and became an expert in making pork sausages. Norman had witnessed him noshing on these wursts, away from his grandmother's watchful eye, when he had visited the store as a youngster. Norman's father, an ophthalmologist, also had this same love affair with hog victuals and had eaten two strips of bacon for breakfast almost every day of his life, but he did draw the line at ham and never ate the forbidden meat on the Jewish high holidays. When Norman and Selma were married, she insisted that they keep a kosher home, and Norman became more observant as the years wore on so that his pig eating eventually caused him considerable anguish.

Norman would sneak out in the noon hour and visit the Rib Shack, a small restaurant in town that was known for its pork ribs, and in thirty minutes he would consume two slabs before returning to work.

On Sundays, he went to the synagogue for the weekly men's club breakfast of lox and bagels, but often left early to patronize the local Denny's for a Grand Slam breakfast with extra sausage and bacon piled on his plate. Every Christmas he received a large ham from one of his patients who was unaware of his religion (even if she didn't know that Kugelman was a Jewish name, his large Semitic nose should have been a clue). He put it in the refrigerator at the office, and in the evening when all the employees had left, he would slice off a big hunk and guiltily devour it before heading home to Selma. Norman attended medical conventions out of town where he would frequent upscale steak houses and order the sixteen-ounce pork chop, while he listened to some expert physician extol the newest product for intestinal gas.

After his pork pig-outs, Norman had sleepless nights dreading that his friends at the synagogue might find out about his salacious desire for the other white meat. He was tempted to make an appointment with the rabbi to discuss his compulsion, but was afraid that the holy man would never hold him in high regard again. He had performed a colonoscopy on Rabbi Horowitz and removed two pre-cancerous polyps, and last year he had cured the rabbi's diarrhea, which seemed to worsen before important sermons to the congregation. At the Yom Kippur service, when it came time to atone for the sin of gluttony, Norman clenched his prayer book and prayed that his addiction might somehow be alleviated. He couldn't confide in Selma, for he feared that her dissatisfaction with him would only worsen, knowing that she came from an orthodox upbringing. Once he had not eaten pork for three weeks, but the next day one of his patients developed a serious complication during a procedure, and after work Norman had wolfed down some "baby back" beauties before arriving home, whereupon he told his wife that he was too distraught to eat dinner.

One day, on his way back from the Rib Shack, Norman was preoccupied with his guilt and didn't see a car turning into the intersection. In retrospect he had probably gone through a red light, but there were no witnesses to corroborate this fact. Norman's small BMW T-boned the other car, and even though he was wearing a seat belt, he suffered a concussion, several cracked ribs, and a punctured lung, as well as a fractured hip. He was rushed to the hospital unconscious and placed on a respirator. While Kugelman was in his obtunded state, he underwent an extracorporeal experience somewhere between earth and the hereafter. An archangel, probably Gabriel (although he didn't give a name), visited him while he was in his stupor, and the good doctor took this opportunity to inquire about his pork addiction. The heavenly being looked benignly at Norman and told him that God no longer had much interest in the dietary laws and while this had been important at the time of Abraham when pigs harbored tape worms, more lethal substances such as cigarettes, booze, and drugs had become the scourges of mankind. Moreover in the past millennium, the Almighty himself had developed a taste for pickled pigs' feet. Gabriel assured the doctor that his hog infatuation would not disqualify him from heaven, but he intended Norman to stay on the earth for several more years.

When he awoke, his nurse, Polly Polk, was the first person that he recognized. She had once assisted him with his colonoscopies before starting work in the intensive care unit. Over the next few weeks he slowly recovered and was transferred to the medical floor before going to the rehab hospital. Polly came to visit him daily, even when he was no longer critical, and she had that encouraging smile and innate cheeriness that most good nurses radiate. When she bent over him to take out his thermometer, he couldn't ignore the scent of her lavender perfume and the slightest cleavage that was exposed by her ample breasts. He spent many afternoons chatting with Polly, and maybe it was the morphine, but he even talked about his out-of-body encounter and his lifelong addiction to pork. She listened intently with a concerned expression, her lustrous blue eyes radiating sympathy. Selma visited daily, and of course she never nagged him while he was recovering, but she did make a nuisance of herself to the hospital staff with her constant carping about the lack of medical attention for her important husband who was on the medical staff of the hospital.

Three months later, Norman returned to his practice, at first part time, but in a few weeks he was carrying a full load. After a while, he noticed that he had lost his yearning for pork. The angel had assuaged his anxiety, and now that he knew that he could eat all the bacon, ham, and ribs that he wished, he had totally lost his cravings. He was on top of the world. His greatest burden had been lifted, and he was a free man.

He rushed to the hospital to tell Polly about his good fortune. He had not seen her since being released from the hospital. When he related the news, she was happy for him and gave him a hug, but even this innocuous gesture stirred a feeling in his groin that he had not experienced in years. He quickly turned and left the intensive care unit, ashamed at the lustful sensation that had possessed him. He lay in bed that night, wide awake, as his mind kept wondering back to the beautiful Polly. At the same time, he was fearful that his wife, friends and rabbi would think him a slimeball if they knew about his lascivious thoughts. He had traded pork for Polly Polk. There is no end to Jewish guilt.

A Colonoscopist's Colonoscopy

I woke up early one winter morning, with beads of sweat breaking out on my forehead. I had a dull aching sensation in my lower gut and a slightly nauseous feeling. Yes, today was the day of my colonoscopy, but I wasn't your average patient. I was usually the colonoscoper, having performed over 25,000 procedures, but today I would be the colonoscopee. As I headed into the bathroom for one last session on the alabaster oval (better known as a toilet seat) and gave one last offering to the god Uranus, I contemplated my predicament. The queasy feeling that I perceived was not just from the laxatives I had taken the night before, but the sense of anxiety that every patient feels prior to undergoing an invasive examination. Yes, this "happy-go-lucky, this won't hurt a bit, you'll be asleep for the whole thing" gastroenterologist was apprehensive about his own colonoscopy. I had no symptoms, but I did have a family history of colon cancer, so a negative result wasn't completely assured. But I had more trepidation about the simple fact that I would be asleep and not in control of the situation. So as I sat there, I reviewed the events that had placed me in this awkward position.

I selected a colleague of mine who did not work at my center to perform the procedure. This prevented the nurses at my unit from having the pleasure of sticking me with an IV and viewing the secret parts of my anatomy. The day before, I had started on my liquid diet and took home the "prep," which consisted of two liters of laxatives. I took the first liter in the early evening, and the taste reminded me of the time I had gone swimming in the Dead Sea and had inadvertently swallowed some of the brine. This horrible palatal sensation must have been avoided by mammals since the Pleistocene Age to prevent sudden expiration. After the ingestion, I experienced a faint rumbling in my gut, which was a slight tremor compared to the full-blown earthquake that was to follow. After a few explosive trips to the commode, I just stayed there, loaded a book on my Kindle, and prepared for a long siege. I drank the second dose later in the evening and finally climbed out of my foxhole around midnight for a few hours of fitful sleep.

As I arose from my toilet seat for the last time, a burning question suddenly entered my consciousness. Why would anyone want to be a gastroenterologist and subject mankind to such an experience? My colleagues and patients have asked me this question many times before, but this time I had to ask this question of myself. I mean if a heart surgeon is the Robert Redford of the medical profession, then the gastroguy is the Ed Norton (remember him from the old Jackie Gleason show?). Because of the shame of belonging to such a lowly profession, I have always tried to deflect my humiliation with poor attempts at humor. "I wanted to be a plumber and couldn't get into plumbing school" was my stock answer for awhile. If I'm in a more cynical mood I'll reply, "I finished last in my class in medical school and this was the best job I could find." I learned never to use that one with a patient. Then I tried, "It was a process of elimination." Lately I've tried a more philosophical aphorism "Most people look ahead in life. I look behind."

But when asking this query of myself, I needed a real answer, and so my entire medical career passed through my mind as my wife drove me to the surgery center. As a medical student, I quickly abandoned obstetrics (I couldn't get up in the middle of the night), surgery (I wasn't able to tie a knot even in Cub Scouts), and psychiatry (too scary). That left me embarking on a career in internal medicine, mostly by default. During my internal medicine residency, I decided I needed to find a subspecialty. I very quickly realized that I was not cut out to be a cardiologist. I found out that people with heart disease could get sick very quickly, and I had to make life-or-death decisions; that was not for me. I never really understood how the lung or kidney worked, so I eschewed them as well. That left me with the liver, stomach, intestine, and colon: the subspecialty of gastroenterology. I was at first more attracted to the liver. We had alcoholics where I trained, and thus a plethora of hepatic disease. This is a stolid as well as solid organ that plods along in the body, and nothing happens very quickly. In those days you couldn't do much to help anybody, but you also couldn't do much harm, and that was fine with me. I mostly looked at lab work and made little noises and grunts in front of patients like "Hmmm," "Aha," and "Yup." When I first started my fellowship, colonoscopy was in its infancy as a diagnostic tool, but it became much more popular after Ronald Regan developed colon cancer and Katy Couric had her colonoscopy televised. In 2000, it was established that regular colonoscopies could prevent colon cancer, and after that I was performing twenty colonoscopies per week.

After executing about a thousand procedures, most gastroenterologists become fairly proficient. The skill level is on par with driving a car; there are occasional hazards ahead, but most of the time it's smooth sailing. Fortunately for me, you can only go one way, and there are no forks in the road. I have a poor sense of direction, which can be attested to by anyone who has ever driven with me. I am one of those talkative types, so as I move through the colon, the nurse, technician, and anesthesiologist must listen to my feckless prattle. How many walruses are living in captivity? How many violin concertos did Beethoven write? Contrary to popular belief, we spend very little time discussing the patient's external anatomy. For one thing, it's dark in the room, and for another, most butts over fifty years of age look about the same, although they come in different sizes. You never heard Darwin mentioning the buttocks of the finch, only the beaks. In my career there have only been two new variations: the completely tanned variety and the flowery tattoo above the crack. But now, the SUV was pulling into the parking lot and, I still had not found my answer.

I signed in, gave my insurance card to the receptionist, and filled out a myriad of forms including consent. I didn't spend much time reviewing the possible complications. I already knew them. It felt strange signing on the patient line, as opposed to the physician space. My doctor came in, and I shook his hand. I was embarrassed that my palm was icy, belying my jovial exterior. We engaged in some small talk, and then he left the room. The nurse came in to start my IV, and I showed her all the large veins in my arm where she could put the needle. She didn't seem too impressed. I tried not to wince when I felt the stick and continued to pretend that the whole thing was no big deal for me. I was wheeled into the procedure room, experienced a little sting in my arm from the anesthetic (propofol of Michael Jackson fame), and fell asleep. I may have had a dream, but I don't remember it.

The next moment, it seemed, I was waking up in the recovery room. My wife was there, and she told me later that I was somewhat loud and obnoxious, telling everyone within ear shot that "I didn't feel a damned thing." The gastrenterologist came in and told me everything had gone well and handed me a copy of my report. I passed lots of gas that had been put in during the procedure (I'm generally good at that), put on my clothes, and headed to Denny's. I rewarded myself with a high-cholesterol dose of bacon and eggs.

The procedure was over, and I had had a successful result. I felt proud that I had actually had the courage to go through the examination that I had recommended to so many patients over the years. There was satisfaction in knowing that my own colon was healthy. The unpleasantness of the preparation has slowly faded in my memory. Maybe preventing cancer and reassuring patients is not such a bad calling in life. I guess I will never know why I chose this profession. After all, I could have been a plumber.

Ode to a Commode

It's just as American as pie à la mode.
The finest accoutrement to any abode.
Your faithful companion if you need to unload.
The welcoming bench from a long trip on the road.
If you leave the seat up your wife calls you a toad,
When you put in too much, it once overflowed.
You might sit for a while if your evacuation has slowed.
The greatest relief if you're going to explode.
There are no rules of etiquette or a dress code.
The porcelain bowl will never corrode.
You can read a small paragraph or the whole episode.
One of the greatest inventions that man has bestowed.

The Goat and the Gastroenterologist

Dr. Sidney Katz retired from gastroenterology when he was sixty-five years old. He had toiled long hours for thirty years in this rather unglamorous specialty, but finally, he was through with looking into stomachs and colons. His departure from the medical profession was done more for his wife Kitty and their two children than for himself, as Sidney didn't have any hobbies, but his wife wanted to live where she could plant an organic garden and smell the bucolic air of the countryside. His daughters had children of their own, and both of their husbands were avid fishermen, as opposed to Sidney, whose ichthyology experience consisted of the pickled herring that he procured at the local delicatessen. The Katzs found ten acres of ground that had a small pond stocked with bass about twenty miles from the city and proximate to his children who resided in the suburbs not far away.

One summer's day, the moving truck came, and by evening, they were ensconced in their new digs. Sidney put on his retirement clothing consisting of a T-shirt and shorts, and as a new landowner, initiated an inspection of the perimeter of his fiefdom. After walking for a while, he was approached by a man from the adjacent property. "I guess you're the new neighbor. My name is Maynard, Maynard Tootlehorn. Glad to have you aboard."

As they shook hands, Sid replied, "I'm Dr. Sidney Katz, but just call me Sid. How much of this land is yours?"

"Oh, I have about fifteen acres. I owned a much larger farm and grew corn for over twenty years, but I turned that over to my son and bought this smaller piece. I began raising goats, and now we make the best cheese in the state, or at least I think we do. Look over there and you'll see my herd." Sidney turned to where Tootlehorn had pointed and observed twenty animals grazing in the pasture. "Goats will eat just about anything, even garbage."

"That reminds me," responded Sidney. "Is there a trash pickup out here?"

"Yep, comes once a week on Wednesdays. Good meeting you, but I have to get those critters in the barn for the night."

Sidney went back into the house and told his wife about Mr. Tootlehorn and the goats that produced cheese. Kitty, always a bit skeptical, retorted, "I've heard they're dirty animals, and I hope they don't stray onto our property." Sidney ignored her pessimism.

The following day, he visited the hardware store and introduced himself to the proprietor. "I bought the house that was for sale on Higby Road, and now I need some garbage cans."

The owner's lined face broke into a smile. "You'll need some sturdy receptacles living in that place," he said and showed him the top of the line containers. Katz didn't understand his comment, but he took the man's advice and headed home in his recently purchased pickup truck. On the evening before the appointed day, Sidney took the cans to the side of the road, as he wasn't exactly sure when the garbage truck would come by, and he wanted to have them out there ready to be emptied.

About six o'clock the next morning, Kitty and Sidney were awakened by a clanking sound. At first they thought the trash truck had arrived, but when they looked outside an hour later, the garbage was strewn all over the road, and the cans were lying on their sides. Sidney remembered bears attacking garbage when they had vacationed in Canada, but he knew there were no such animals in their area, so he presumed it might have been a dog. The Katzs cleaned up the garbage and swept the remnants off the road. The same scenario occurred the next week, so the following Wednesday, they awoke at the crack of dawn to discover the culprit. To their surprise, a goat sauntered over from Tootlehorn's property and proceeded to knock a container over by butting it, and when the top flew off, she stuck her head inside, pulled apart a plastic bag, started munching on orange peels, and even swallowed some of the coffee grounds, filter and all.

At this point, Sidney ran out yelling at the goat, but the animal scarcely moved and kept chewing. He hustled over to the Tootlehorn house and knocked on the door. Maynard answered. The doctor yelled, "Get your goat out of my garbage!" Tootlehorn responded in a light-hearted tone, "Don't let the goat get your goat." Sidney didn't laugh at this attempt at a joke, but glared at his neighbor until he came out of the house with an old halter and wrapped it around the creature's neck and pulled her away. "Gertrude produces the best milk of the lot, and she's the number one garbage eater at our house." He didn't seem remorseful or apologetic in any way.

Sidney began making trips into town to buy supplies, and he often stopped at the local coffee shop before going home, mostly out of boredom, but soon he became acquainted with the local professionals who frequented the place. One morning, he struck up a conversation with Byron Smoot, the local vet who had heard that Sidney was a retired gastroenterologist. "You know, last month I saw two horses that just wouldn't eat, and we had to send them to the university where they looked into their stomachs with a scope and found that they had ulcers. Maybe if I purchased a secondhand instrument, with your training, you could show me how to use it." Sidney jumped at this suggestion, as he had many open dates on his calendar with nothing much to occupy his time. He called up his old salesman, and soon there was a serviceable apparatus in the office of Dr. Smoot.

A few days later, the vet called Sidney with the following story. An elderly St. Bernard had come to the office, and his owner complained that the dog was vomiting on a daily basis and had lost several pounds. The next day, Smoot put the dog under anesthesia while the GI doctor entered his stomach, and sure enough, he found severe gastritis probably from the ibuprofen that the dog had been taking for arthritis in his hind hips. The following week, they scoped a pig and soon Sidney was spending one afternoon a week looking into the innards of pets and livestock. The other vets in the area heard of his skill and started sending their animals to the clinic for the procedure.

Meanwhile, things were going pretty well on the Katz farm. Kitty's garden began to yield results, and they relished the home-grown produce. Sidney still sorely missed his old job, but passed the time exploring the wooded area on the property and fishing with his grandkids. However, garbage tampering continued to be a problem. The erstwhile doctor placed a lock around the cans, but the goat was still able to knock them over, and finally he built a fence to encompass the receptacles, hoping that would solve the problem. One day, he was out in the yard and noticed Maynard dumping a bag of kitchen scraps out his back door for his goats to eat. Sidney abruptly understood that the cheese maker was intentionally feeding his critters garbage, believing that this produced a better grade of chevre.

After a while, the Katzs decided to do some remodeling and hired a contractor to put in a new kitchen and bathroom and also add a bedroom to the upper floor, which had previously been an attic. In the upstairs room, they discovered some old farm equipment including some harnesses, rope, and an ancient cowbell. Kitty wanted to keep some of the stuff, thinking that one day it might be worth something, but Sidney convinced her to throw it all in the trash. At daybreak, they heard the dreaded dissonance of metallic objects. To their shock, Gertrude had dug a hole under the fence and was peacefully chowing down their refuse. It was then that Sidney decided to hire a lawyer and sue Tootlehorn for trespassing.

The next day, he knocked on the farmer's door intending to threaten him with the lawsuit, when he noticed a worried look on the old man's face. "Gertrude threw up all night and wouldn't eat or drink anything this morning, and I can't figure out what's wrong with the old girl. I might have to take her into Doc Smoot. I can't afford to lose Gertrude just when she's in her milk-producing prime." Katz realized this wasn't the time to disclose his intentions, so he just grunted and walked away.

That afternoon he got a call from the vet. "Sid, could you come down here right away? I've got Maynard Tootlehorn's prize goat in here. She's dehydrating from vomiting, and I think she needs an emergency scope." Sid thought about saying no, his disgust for the goat owner was that strong, but he heard himself saying, "OK, Byron, I'll be right there."

When he arrived at the office, Gertrude was lying on the operating table sedated, with an IV already in place. He plugged the instrument into the light source, put some lubricant on the end of the scope, and gently placed it in the goat's mouth. He expertly passed it through the upper sphincter and into the esophagus, which contained a large amount of saliva and other secretions. Sidney suctioned the fluid and was on his way toward the stomach, but not quite. As he reached the bottom of the esophagus, he saw a piece of metal glinting in the distance, and as he got closer, he could make out some lettering, "MADE IN USA 1952," and then he could see the outline of the object. It was the cowbell he had discarded the day before, and it had impacted in the distal end of the goat's gullet. He asked the nurse to hand him a snare, which projected out of the scope like a lasso, and after several tries, he was able to get it around the clapper and pulled it snug. He gently removed the scope, and the bell followed, attached to the snare. There appeared to be some mild trauma to the lining of the esophagus, but no perforation had occurred, and fifteen minutes later, Gertrude was awake and happily lapping water from a bowl.

Sidney and Byron walked into the waiting room where Maynard was anxiously waiting, and they showed him the item that his goat had swallowed. "I'm mighty grateful for your good work, Sid. I guess old Gertrude bit off more than she could chew," he joked with an audible chuckle. Byron laughed, but Sidney replied somewhat sternly, "That's what you get for feeding your goats garbage; you never know what they'll devour." Suddenly the old farmer stood up and hugged him, and Sidney could see that Maynard had tears in his eyes. "You're right; I made a stupid mistake. Without that goat my business would be in trouble. Thanks for saving her life!"

The next garbage day, all was silent. Sidney and Kitty looked out from their window and saw Gertrude grazing in the pasture, making no attempt to squeeze under the fence, even though the hole was still present. It seemed that she had learned her lesson; whatever was in their garbage she never wanted to consume again. After that, Katz and Tootlehorn became close friends, and when the old farmer needed some capital to expand his business, he made Sidney a partner. The doctor forgot all about the practice of medicine and left the animal scoping to Dr. Smoot, who had been an apt pupil. Soon the retired gastroenterologist was raising goats on his own property. Kitty lost her aversion to the creatures and started feeding them vegetables that she had grown in her garden. With Maynard's help and Sidney's knowledge of the digestive system, they developed an award-winning cheese, "Dr. Katz's Organic Goat Cheese with Probiotics," which they touted for individuals with digestive problems. Sidney had found his calling after retirement, and none of the goats ever ate garbage again.

Golfing with My Dad

I recently celebrated my fiftieth anniversary of playing golf. I took up the game when I was thirteen years old, and now I am in my mid-sixties. My dad would take me to the public course in Falcon Lake, Manitoba, where we spent the summer. Actually, there was very little of that season, and the weather was only conducive to golfing from June to early September. It started to snow in October. The layout was cut from the Canadian Shield, which is mostly rock and trees; grass was a foreign substance in that area. There were swarms of large mosquitoes in July and nasty, biting black flies in August. The dragonflies were as large as sparrows. There were no tee times in those days, and the course was crowded with players who often brought small children or pets with them. My dad would drag me out of bed about 4:30 a.m. (the summer days were exceptionally long in that part of North America), and we would put our names in with the pro and hope to get off around eight a.m. We wouldn't be done for another five or six hours.

My father was a terrible golfer, but he completely eschewed professional instruction, even though he loved the sport. I think he believed that if he didn't improve after lessons, then he would have to admit to himself that the game was too hard for him. On the other hand, if he never took a lesson, he always had an excuse for his poor play. He had an exceedingly short backswing. He would take the club back about two feet with a wrist cock, get into a crouch, and then take a vicious swipe at the ball. About ninety percent of the time this would result in either a horrible chunk or a vicious top, but about one swing in ten would establish solid contact, and the ball would travel amazingly far. Occasionally, we would get paired up with an accomplished golfer and my dad would tell me he had a "grooved swing." He didn't tell me how you could acquire this proficiency, but clearly in our family the grooved swing was not obtainable. Obviously my dad was not a great role model for the fundamentals of golf.

The "no-lesson rule" also applied to me. Practicing was also forbidden. I believe that he didn't want me to become too adept at the game for fear I would turn into a "golf bum"; I would spend too much time at the course and neglect my studies, and even though I might learn to be a good golfer, I would be a complete failure in life and not amount to anything.

I started off with a cheap second-hand set of clubs and tried to adapt my baseball swing to a golf swing. Even with this unorthodox swing, I had high expectations of my golf ability and an extremely bad temper if things didn't go well. I can remember slamming my putter several inches into the green after missing a short putt, to the complete mortification of my father. I was also very impatient in those dreadfully slow rounds and couldn't wait for the group ahead of us to get out of range before I teed it up. Invariably, I would hit the best shot of the day and almost bean the people in front of us with the ball. On more than one occasion a red-faced fellow would come running up to us swinging his club like a tomahawk, and my poor, embarrassed dad would have to apologize for me. "He's just a kid."

As I got older, I became occupied with my medical studies and only played a few rounds of mediocre golf per year. My parents left Canada and retired to Palm Springs, California, the golf mecca of the world. My mother became enthused with the sport and began to golf with him. When I was forty-six years old, my wife and I divorced, and I took up the game more seriously as a way to pass some time and block out the turmoil in my life. I realized that I needed lessons in order to improve, and that most good golfers swing similarly with a few variations. Soon I was breaking 90 with some regularity, and after a few years, I was shooting under 85 and even scored in the 70s a number of times.

I began to spend more time with my dad, who by then was in his late seventies. He was still playing golf three days a week. His swing was exactly the same. Even though the country club had a beautiful driving range, on no occasion would he use it for practice or for warming up prior to a round. He refused to line up a putt or take out the flag stick on the green. After completing the hole, he immediately went back into the cart and waited for my mother to finish putting. He took great delight in my improvement as a golfer and was eager to hear about my rounds. I tried to give him some tips to improve his game, but he failed to follow any of them. He constantly complained about the sluggish pace of the people in front of us. He would tell me, "We have a bunch of old guys holding us up." I never pointed out to him that he was in the same age group.

My dad passed away eleven years ago. We played our last round together in 2000. His kidneys were failing, but his spirits were good, and he didn't spend much time discussing his illness. He could only drive the ball about 150 yards and became indignant when I suggested the senior tees. I knew that our time together was coming to an end. It wasn't until he was no longer on this earth that I realized how much I loved golfing with him. Your golf buddies may want you to play well, but not as well as them. It's only your dad who enjoys your good shot more than you do.

Now, as my retirement age approaches, I look forward to the days when I can play more golf, particularly at senior rates. Unfortunately my skills are diminishing as I get older, although the enthusiasm for the game still burns within me. I'm still hoping to hit that great shot or sink the long putt. I no longer have my dad, but my son has taken up the game, and I recently became a grandfather. I don't think I'll use the same approach that he used. I'll encourage practice and instruction, and I won't be concerned about them playing too much. The only golf bum in the family will be me.

The Feeding Tube

Mrs. Gladys Johnson was an elderly patient with chronic ulcerative colitis whom I had treated for many years. She had been a school psychologist and was an avid reader and golfer. Her husband, an ophthalmologist, had died a number of years previously. Her disease was quite manageable, and during her visits, we spent most of the time talking politics, golf, or the state of medicine today as opposed to a number of years ago when her husband had been in practice. She had three children: Victoria, Carl, and Reginald. Vicky was quite devoted to her mother and lived only a few blocks from her. She was a nurse and worked at the hospital where I had privileges, and I had known her for a number of years. To his parents' regret, the middle child, Carl, had dropped out of college and was intermittently unemployed. He suffered from depression and chronic back pain. Reginald was clearly the favorite. He was a brilliant student and had obtained a doctorate in mathematics at an Ivy League school. He took a position on Wall Street and eventually became very wealthy, managing a hedge fund. His mother's only regret was that he visited infrequently, and she felt uncomfortable visiting him in his lavish home in Greenwich, Connecticut.

Last year Gladys made an appointment to see me, but on this occasion I was surprised that Vicky had accompanied her to the office. I had not seen Gladys for about a year and, in that time, I could see a definite personality change. She was surprisingly quiet and detached. Vicky did most of the talking. She was concerned that her mother had lost twenty pounds over the last four months.

When I questioned Gladys about this, she told me that her appetite was fine, but she just felt full after eating. Vicky also mentioned that her mother had acted strangely on a few occasions. On her ladies' Wednesday golf outing, she had driven the golf cart onto the putting green, to the horror of her partners, and she was so embarrassed that she had given up golf. One day when Vicky was visiting, Gladys tried to turn on the TV with her cell phone and insisted it was the remote. While Vicky was relating these stories, Gladys just sat there with a distant look and a slight smile on her face. Her physical examination and routine blood tests were normal, and I concluded that she was in the early phase of Alzheimer's disease. I related my suspicions of early dementia to Vicky and sent a letter to her internist.

Six months later, Gladys was admitted to the hospital with pneumonia. She had lost more weight, and her confusion had worsened. A swallowing study revealed a small amount of aspiration. Her doctor wanted my opinion about placing a feeding tube. When I entered her room, I was dismayed at the change in her. She was pitifully thin. She seemed to recognize me, but could not remember my name or the name of the hospital. Carl and Vicky were at her bedside with the stunned sadness of children when they see their parent failing. I explained to them that while the feeding tube could prolong her life, it might not improve the quality of the time left to her. Carl asked if the tube feeding would help her gain weight, and I told him this was probable, but it wouldn't bring back her memory. Vicky didn't say much, but I knew that as a nurse these options were depressing. Carl and Vicky told me they would talk it over and let me know. When I asked about Reginald, they apprised me that he had to settle some business affairs and would be flying in by private jet. He hadn't seen his mother for about a year, and they were confident that he would go along with their decision.

The following day was Friday, and I came by to see Gladys that afternoon. The IV fluids and antibiotics had improved her condition, and she appeared more alert. Vicky and Carl were present. They had decided to place her in a nursing home with hospice care and forgo the feeding tube. I told them that I knew it was a difficult decision, but I agreed with their plan. I signed off her case.

Early Monday I received a call from Reginald who had landed in town over the weekend. He notified me that he was very upset that judgments had been made without his consent. In a very imperious tone, he demanded another conference that morning. I told him that I was seeing office patients, but I would come by on rounds that afternoon. When I arrived at the hospital, I saw Reginald attending to his mother, trying to get her to sip some Ensure. His eyes were red and swollen, and apparently he had been crying. The other children were at the foot of her bed with melancholy expressions. Reginald left his mother and strode over to me to introduce himself. It was obvious that he was a man who was accustomed to being in charge. He made it very clear that he did not agree with his siblings' decision and believed that it was malpractice to let his mother starve to death, and, of course, the tube should be placed. He thought that with hydration and nutrition his mother could get stronger and begin to swallow normally again. My prognosis had been much too pessimistic. He advised me that if I didn't place the tube, he would consult another gastroenterologist.

I looked over at Carl and Vicky, and they had guilty looks as if to say they were sorry that they had ever thought of letting their mother perish from lack of nutrition. At this point, I knew that a repeat discussion of the pros and cons of the feeding tube would not be helpful. The next day I inserted the gastrostomy tube, and Gladys was discharged to the nursing home the following day.

Several months passed, and I forgot about Gladys Johnson until I bumped into Vicky at the hospital. She informed me that her mother had died three weeks previously. She had fractured her hip at the home and had been confined to a wheelchair. Shortly thereafter, she had been admitted for recurrent pneumonia and urinary tract infection. Her last sojourn to the hospital was for congestive heart failure. The family had been at the bedside when she died. I inquired if Reginald had also been present, and a distressed look came across her face. No, she had only seen Reginald one other time since our meeting. He had flown in for the funeral.

The Substandard Standard Poodle

My name is Jack, and I am a dog. I have lived at the home of Dave and Laura for ten years and have reached the age of thirteen, which is quite elderly for a canine. I am not particularly smart for a poodle. In fact I'm not smart at all. Dave tells me I'm about the dumbest dog he has ever owned.

My first masters became bored with me. Filling my feeding bowl and taking me out to relieve myself were chores that eventually took their toll on this older couple, and one day they took me to the groomer and left me there. Laura came by the next day and the proprietor asked her to board me, if only for a few days until they could find a permanent placement.

When I arrived at their home, I observed that this was another middle-aged tandem with no kids, and there were two other standard poodles already at the place. I thought my chances of staying there for longer than a week were slim, but I decided to put my best paw forward. I couldn't wow my new friends with clever tricks (because I don't know any), but I ate the kibble that was set out for me, emptied my bowels and bladder at the appropriate times, and came into the house when I was called. Above all, I made no sounds for the first several weeks, for I have a very shrill and irritating bark. Some dogs have a cadence to their barking which can impress people and even scare strangers, but I have a monotonous yap, and Dave has informed me more than once that he would rather be at the dentist undergoing a root canal than listen for more than two minutes to my repetitive oral emissions. I soon realized that Laura was a very compassionate person, and she took pity on me. After only a few days, she told me I could live with them forever. Dave was skeptical about owning a third dog, and he sensed that I had been on my most exemplary behavior, but he went along with Laura.

At my previous abode I had only eaten dog chow, and I had never experienced a treat. You can imagine my exhilaration when I was given my first piece of cheese. After dinner, the other dogs were told to sit as Dave meted out the slices of cheddar. I wasn't acquainted with this ritual, but I sat in line with my fellow canines. After my first mouthful of the golden curd, a wondrous sensation reverberated from my palate to my brain, and like many others of my species, I became addicted. I'll eat Stilton or Gouda, Colby or Swiss but most of the time they give me the off-label American that can be found at any grocery store (Dave is known to be pretty frugal). I'll start pawing Dave in the evening to remind him of my craving. He eventually gets up after a few curses and opens the refrigerator to get the cheese. This gets me very excited, and I start my staccato barking, which even aggravates Laura, who is always my defender. After I eat my ration (one slice per dog), I settle down and begin to dream of my next encounter with the lustrous substance. Often because my memory is unusually short, I will forget that I just had my treat and start pestering Dave again; this leads to further epithets and then Laura admonishes Dave about his obscenities, but she will sneak more cheese to me after Dave has gone to bed. This scenario is repeated daily, but unlike humans, each day is a new experience for me, as I really can't recall the day before or the day before that.

The oldest poodle is Elmo. He's an indoor dog. He only goes out to relieve himself and then heads back into the house. He prefers air-conditioning in the summer and the warmth of the furnace in the winter. Elmo is very intelligent and relishes watching television. He doesn't like to roughhouse and chase around the furniture with the other dogs. Sometimes he will sneak up on me and stick his nose near my private parts and start sniffing. I find that exceedingly annoying. Bernie, the third poodle, is my buddy. He is a big husky guy with a broad nose and large brown eyes. He spends much of his day looking out the window and barking at the people who walk by our house. He has a deep, husky growl which would frighten any passerby, but he never realizes that they can't hear him when he is inside the house. When he gets into one of his paroxysms, Dave or Laura will put him in his crate, but the funny thing is that he likes the crate, so it doesn't stop him from barking again as soon as he is liberated. Elmo and Bernie also delight in jumping up on a chair and licking the evening dinner plates, which gets Dave swearing a blue streak and yelling at Laura that "her" dogs are poorly behaved.

I love the outdoors. My owners release me into the backyard four or five times per day. This is the second stimulus to my agonizing jackhammer barking. I feel sorry about tormenting Dave and Laura with my canine explosions, but, unfortunately, I can't help myself. Even though I've been let out into the same enclosure five times per day for ten years (about eighteen thousand trips), each sojourn is a new experience, which overwhelms my small cerebrum and causes uncontrollable eruptions of pleasure.

I love to sniff along the back of the property. In this area I can pick up the scents of rabbits and opossums that inhabit the small wooded area beyond the fence. Even though I've only caught one baby rabbit in all the years I've been searching (Dave said it was already dead when I found it, but he's wrong), the hunt is never boring. Another section of fence borders on a neighboring dwelling, and I can spend hours smelling the exquisite excretions of their small Shitzu. I don't mind if my fur gets saturated from rain or my paws become caked in mud. After thirty or sixty minutes in these worthwhile endeavors, I will hear the melodious voice of Laura, or the rather harsh commandments of Dave, calling me back inside. I reluctantly trot through the door to await my next adventure into my amazing universe.

Once I return to the house, I enjoy snoozing in my doggie bed. I seem to sleep more as I get older. I start with my pre-breakfast and post-breakfast naps followed by midmorning, pre-lunch, post-lunch, midafternoon, and pre- and post-dinner siestas, but if I hear that backdoor start to open, I have the ability to suddenly wake up, run to the exit, and immediately start my shrill, incessant yammering.

That's all I can tell you about my life as a substandard standard poodle. I wish I could exhibit all the dog shtick that I know or all the blue ribbons that I have won, but I can't. I know that Laura loves me for who I am. She never forgets to put food in my bowl, take me to the groomer, or schedule my veterinary appointments. She praises me daily and tells me I'm a good puppy, although those years are long behind me. Even stony-hearted Dave will sometimes lie on the sofa with me and rub the top of my head until I fall asleep, and I hope that when I am gone, he will miss me and maybe forget that I was the dumbest dog he ever owned.

River of Fire

I first met Bill in 2000, when he was hospitalized for gastrointestinal complaints and liver dysfunction related to alcoholism. I was the gastroenterologist on call that day, and as Bill had no health coverage, I was assigned to his care. When I arrived on the ward, I inquired as to his bed assignment, and the gruff ward secretary responded, "The drunk is in 521."As I entered the room, I saw a Caucasian male of slight build, unkempt, with the course tremors of alcohol withdrawal. He was fifty-three at the time but looked considerably older. His complexion was sallow, his face prematurely wrinkled, his mouth edentulous, and he smelled of stale whiskey, but strangely, his horned-rim glassed gave him an odd, professorial appearance. He complained of abdominal pain and vomiting and freely admitted to downing a fifth of bourbon daily. He seemed eager to talk, and his story was tragic.

Bill's parents divorced when he was thirteen, and the following year his father was killed in a hit-and-run accident on Christmas Eve. His mother was a lush, and after his father's death, Bill started to drink while suffering physical abuse from his stepfather. When he was seventeen, he was present when his mother was shot dead by a boyfriend, and the gun was then turned on Bill, but it jammed, and he chased the murderer from the house. Bill and an older brother were left to raise their four younger siblings, two of whom became alcoholics and suffered premature deaths.

He dropped out of high school, married, and three daughters were born in rapid succession. Bill entered the service and studied electronics before going to Vietnam, where he claimed to have suffered from post-traumatic stress, but, as he told it, his records "got screwed up" and somehow he was never eligible for military benefits. He earned his GED in the Army, and after discharge, he went to college and attained a 3.7 grade point average while working and supporting his wife and children. Bill obtained a well-paying job at a large multinational corporation, but was subsequently fired after he got into a dispute with management over some defective parts.

After that, he never held a steady job, and his boozing became an addiction. His first wife left town on Thanksgiving Day 1982, and his daughters were placed in foster homes after one of them accused him of child abuse. He married his current wife, Janice, the next year. He had been in three inpatient alcohol rehabilitation programs, and the longest he was ever dry was eighteen months.

After a few days in hospital, his symptoms subsided, and he was ready for discharge. Because of his lack of medical insurance, he could not find a primary care doctor, so I agreed to take him on as a patient, but I was fairly certain—like many inebriates I had treated in the past—that he would not keep his appointment. I told him to return in two weeks, with the usual stern warnings about the risk of death if his imbibing persisted, and he promised that he would restart his Alcoholics Anonymous meetings.

To my surprise, he arrived at the scheduled time. He appeared forlorn and dejected and told me that despite his best intentions, he had resumed his love affair with the Wild Turkey. His brutal honesty about his wretched predicament intrigued me as a physician, and I felt that there might be a slight chance that I could help him. I started an antidepressant and encouraged him to continue his efforts to abstain, but the absence of health benefits precluded further assistance. Soon after, he suffered a small cerebral hemorrhage, and this may have frightened him enough so that he stopped drinking for several months.

I began to enjoy Bill's visits. I found out that he liked to write poetry and had started two novels. He had done some painting and wood carving and was an avid gardener when the devils in his mind weren't in control, and I realized there was a talented man underneath the shroud of whiskey.

Bill started missing appointments and then stopped coming altogether, and I became suspicious that he had fallen off the wagon. My misgivings were confirmed when he turned up in the office two years later. He was hallucinating and thought that his mother was in the exam room with us, and he was obviously jaundiced, a sign of a failing liver.

He was admitted to the hospital in a delirious state and was diagnosed with the encephalopathy of liver disease. His wife was no longer able to care for him, and he was transferred to a nursing home under hospice care, but miraculously his liver improved off the liquor, and he was able to return home and became the rare patient that ever left that service without dying. The following year, he requested to be evaluated for a liver transplant and was seen at the university, but was turned down because of his recurrent drinking and previous stroke. He began to quaff again and had further bouts of confusion.

In 2006, he had another dry period. He brought me some tomatoes and cucumbers from his garden, and I shared them with my staff. I joked that this was bartering for my fee, as I had received scant remuneration for being his doctor. Through 2007, he kept off the bottle and remained productive.

One day, I received a three-page letter from Bill. It was somewhat rambling, but his handwriting was meticulous, and there were some passages of lucid insight into his character. He realized that he was cursed with the twin afflictions of depression and alcoholism, but he felt he was putting his life together and was even planning to write a book about his experiences. He was appreciative that I had not abandoned him, and wrote, "You saw that flicker of life in me and that tiny flame has become a river of fire."

Several months later, there was a real fire at their home, and Bill's melancholia resurfaced. By the end of 2008, he was imbibing again, and when I saw him in the clinic he was shaky, disoriented, and the jaundice had reappeared. He refused hospital admission and expressed a desire to die, and sadly, I realized the inevitability of that wish. I no longer felt the need to warn him about further risks to his health—he knew them as well as me—and I even feigned some hollow optimism.

Despite my gloomy assessment, he beat back his cerebral goblins for a time and even raised some vegetables in 2010 despite developing severe alcoholic neuropathy, which necessitated use of a walker. His last visit was early in 2011. He had turned sixty-five, and in our bizarre health care system, he had joined a Medicare Advantage Plan and was required to leave me for a physician who accepted that insurance. He was very cheerful that day, and he and his faithful wife expressed their gratitude for the assistance that I had provided over the years.

Early in 2012, Bill resumed his enduring obsession with booze. He fell at home, hit his head, and a few days later became unresponsive. He was brought by ambulance to the emergency room and placed on a ventilator. Janice called to tell me the distressing news, and I visited Bill in the intensive care unit, more as a friend than as a physician, and concurred with her decision to discontinue the life-support systems. Shortly thereafter, Bill's presence on this earth came to a humble end. Hopefully his anguished soul is now at peace.

As I drove home from the hospital that evening, my mind was on Bill, and I thought to myself how my life might have evolved if fate had dealt me those DNA strands of toxic genes wrapped around a completely dysfunctional family. I recalled my privileged childhood and the loving memories of my deceased parents. Success is the combination of persistence, plus a fair amount of luck, and it was the luck part that Bill never received. He had spent most of his tortured existence battling his demons, and for a time I believed he had conquered them. But ultimately the demons had won, and his river of fire had finally been doused by one last bottle of bourbon.

The Lump

Ms. Crump was a frump, who was exceedingly plump,
And because she was plump, she had a large rump.
One day on her rump, she perceived a small lump,
So she saw Dr. Klump for the small lump on her rump.
But the rump of Ms. Crump was so exceedingly plump,
That Klump could not feel the small lump on her rump.
This caused her to grump and she left with a humph,
While the dumped Dr.Klump slumped like a chump.
On the way home, the frump caught her pump on a stump,
And flumped with a whump on her rump that was plump.
A painful hump appeared on her rump from the thump,
Which elicited a jump if her rump she did bump.
Ms. Crump forgot all about the very small lump
But she never returned to the good Dr. Klump.

Jewish Christmas Songs

Christmas has never been my favorite time of year. Some Jews substitute Hanukkah, but it has never worked for me. Like most people, I listen to the annual Christmas renditions that are blared incessantly on almost every radio station throughout the season, but it was only recently that I discovered the strong Jewish connection to the yuletide favorites. Mel Torme and Bob Wells, Jewish boys in their early twenties, wrote "The Christmas Song" in thirty-five minutes on a hot summer day in Los Angeles. I'm willing to bet they never roasted any chestnuts on an open fire, and in California, they would rarely experience Jack Frost nipping at their Semitic noses. I guess if they ever visited a church, they might have seen "Yuletide carols sung by a choir," but I doubt that they ever witnessed "folks dressed up like Eskimos." "White Christmas" is another classic. It was written by Irving Berlin, whose real name was Israel Isidore Baline, son of a kosher butcher, who grew up on the lower East Side of New York. It's unlikely that he had much familiarity with "treetops that glisten" or "children listen to hear sleigh bells in the snow".

For the past twenty years, I have taken call for my physician partners on the Christian holy day. As I roll out of bed that morning, I glance out the window hoping the streets won't be icy for the trip to the hospital. I'm certainly not humming the tune, "Let it Snow! Let it Snow! Let it Snow!" written by the Jewish duo of Sammy Cahn and Jule Styne. On my way to the hospital, I marvel at the lack of traffic at seven in the morning, and I try to imagine the destination of the few cars that are on the road on that day at that hour. I doubt that any of them contain lawyers, accountants, or business people; they're still snuggled between the sheets, dreaming about the gifts that Santa might bring them. Maybe the occupants are going home from a raucous time of all-night partying, or getting up early to see their grandchildren open gifts, or looking for a store that's open to buy a loaf of bread or a quart of milk. I could empathize with a fireman in a fire truck, but I've never seen a fire on Christmas Day. Soon I'm obsessing over the delusion that nobody except me is going to work on that day. "I'll Be Home for Christmas" by Walter Kent (born Walter Kauffman) and Buck Ram is certainly not a song that I'll want to hear on the car stereo at that moment.

As a kid, I always felt like a misfit during the holiday season. Lighting the Hanukkah candles and watching them melt was the most excitement that took place at our house. I found that spinning a dreidel was a dull way to pass the time, and that was well before the advent of video games. Potato latkes have always given me indigestion. There was never a thought in my mind that "Santa Claus is Coming to Town" (a song written by Fred Coots, religion unknown, but first sung by Eddie Cantor, born Edward Israel Iskowitz). When other youngsters were scanning the heavens looking for "Rudolph the Red Nosed Reindeer," written by Jewish composer Johnny Marks, I was in bed fast asleep. In the 60s, there were only three television channels, and all I can remember is the pope officiating at Christmas Mass. I guess it must have been rerun several times during the day. Recently, Pope Benedict performed the Mass at ten p.m., so he wouldn't have to stay up past midnight. My abode must have differed greatly from that of Al Stillman (born Albert Silverman), who wrote "There's No Place like Home for the Holidays."

Around the middle of December, many gentiles ask each other, "Are you ready for Christmas?" and I have been posed that question on many occasions by acquaintances who don't know I'm Jewish. At first I tried to explain that I didn't celebrate the holiday, but the person making the inquiry seemed so taken aback by my unexpected answer that I stopped responding that way several years ago. Now I tell them, "I am absolutely one hundred percent ready for Christmas, and I have done every bit of my Christmas shopping." I might even sing the refrain written by Felix Bernard, "to face unafraid the plans that we made walking in a Winter Wonderland." The questioner usually tells me how lucky I am to have completed my purchases, as opposed to her (often a nurse) predicament in not having completed the task.

I've encountered a number of patients who become depressed at Christmastime. They often complain of spending time with relatives that they don't like or not spending time with relatives they do like. Some have memories of loved ones who are deceased and can no longer celebrate with them. There can be a financial strain if they don't have money to buy gifts for their children or grandchildren. Not uncommonly, people exhaust themselves hosting the holiday gathering; others dread being alone on the special day. Obviously not everyone shares the sentiments of George Wyle (born Bernard Weissman) who wrote, "It's the Most Wonderful Time of the Year," or the ubiquitous Johnny Marks who composed "A Holly Jolly Christmas." The syrupy optimistic lyrics of "Silver Bells," written by Jay Livingstone (born Jacob Levinson) and Ray Evans, might not appeal to those who are feeling lugubrious on the yuletide.

Come to think of it, maybe Jews are more fortunate than Christians in not having to endure the stress of the Christmas season. There is no pressure on us to buy gifts, have parties, or visit with obnoxious relatives. The pang of self-pity that I reserve for myself driving to work on that day is minor compared to the angst suffered by some Christians. Maybe Jewish composers wrote those sappy, happy tunes because they only experienced Christmas as outsiders. After all, the saddest song that I hear on the holiday is Elvis Presley's rendition of "Blue Christmas," and that was written by two gentiles, Billy Hayes and Jay Johnson.

The Great Grocery Adventure

For most of my life, the grocery store was a place that I seldom frequented, but last year I received a cookbook for my birthday, and I decided to undertake a biweekly pilgrimage to our neighborhood supermarket to obtain nutrients for my family. As a practicing gastroenterologist, I had always had an appreciation for healthy eating, but obtaining and preparing food was something I had never attempted. In St. Louis where I live, the most popular grocery chain is Schnucks. When I first moved to the city, I thought the name was a Jewish joke, a cross between the Yiddish words *schnook* (translation: jerk) and *schmuck* (translation: real jerk), but after a short time I learned that Schnuck was the last name of the founder of the company.

Before departing for the market, the serious shopper needs to prepare a list of things to buy, and I've learned that it's important to check the pantry to be sure that the ingredients aren't already there before making any purchases. Unfortunately, at our house I never know where anything is kept because my wife is constantly rearranging all the items in the kitchen. It's disheartening to return home with a fresh jar of coriander or marjoram only to find that these items already exist in some drawer, and then she tells me it will take fifteen years before we will use up what we already have, and usually I'm too lazy to take the new stuff back. Being a doctor, I have taken pride in my illegible handwriting (ask any nurse in my office), but unlike a patient's prescription, which is deciphered by a diligent pharmacist, it's extremely important that my itinerary is legible so that I don't bring home a scallion instead of a scallop, a parsnip instead of parsley, or a quince instead of quinoa.

My Schnucks is situated in a large strip mall in suburbia Americana. As an absent-minded person with a poor sense of direction, I have been embarrassed on more than one occasion by not being able to find my car in the parking lot upon leaving the building. You may be able to wander around with a small package and make people think you are on your way to another establishment in the mall, but if you're pushing a grocery cart, most observers will know that your automobile is lost. After a few months, I noticed that the light poles have numerals on them to mark the rows, and I try to remember which digit is proximate to my car.

After I select my cart and ascertain that it is in working order, I begin my circumnavigation of the store. My first stop is usually the produce section. One must be very careful when buying apples, pears, or peaches. Initially I would choose any odd piece of fruit, pop them into a cellophane bag, and take them home, but later as I was about to eat the specimen I would notice some disfigurement—a bruise or brown spot that I had not appreciated at the market. Now I inspect each piece, jousting with the other housewives and househusbands at the fruit bins, searching for blemishes or nodules similar to the way a dermatologist examines skin or a urologist feels a prostate. Regrettably, I am still unable to sniff a cantaloupe and know that it's ripe, but I hope to acquire that skill in the near future. I approach the vegetables with trepidation. I really enjoy Brussels sprouts, but several months ago I bought a large quantity of the small cabbages and cooked them with an inappropriate amount of garlic, and I produced enough gas that evening to power a small hot air balloon. Then there is the lowly rutabaga, a brown ugly specimen that looks like a large turd, and so far I've been unsuccessful in finding a recipe that will unlock its hidden flavor. Beets are difficult for me. They're often covered in mud, hard to peel, and will turn your urine a magenta color which you might mistake for blood.

The deli section has a prominent place in most groceries. At first I didn't realize that I needed to take a number and just ambled up to the front of the counter, but then some mother with four kids in tow gave me a dirty look and pointed to the back of the line while waving her ticket at me. Now I meekly take a number, find my place in the rear, and study the varieties of sliced turkey available: the all-natural golden roasted turkey, the mesquite-flavored smoked turkey, the holiday-cured barbecue turkey, or the Vermont maple golden turkey. Because of the mental difficulty in making a selection, I tend to get the same brand: the apple-wood honey-cured, cracked peppercorn, oven-hearth, low-sodium turkey.

There is a huge section of bottled water, and I counted thirteen different brands on display. I found that Poland Spring is not water from Poland but from the Poland Spring in Maine, but much of the water comes from Fryeburg, Maine, not Poland. The Dasani and Aquafina are major players, and they honestly admit that their water comes from municipal sources, i.e. tap water. Now why would anybody pay for tap water when you can get it out of the faucet for free? Then there is Ice Mountain, which is obtained from springs in Pennsylvania but not from Ice Mountain, which is in West Virginia. Fiji water is obtained from the island of Fiji. The company pays a tax to the Fijians, so that the water can be distributed to poor people who don't have access to clean water. You might think that everybody on the island could drink clean water before they export it eight thousand miles away. All the brands carry a label indicating that there are no calories in the water, which proves the obvious point. You can't get fat drinking water. I decide that I will continue to obtain my water from "municipal sources."

I move on to the snack section; this takes up several aisles and there are rows and rows of crackers, pretzels, and chips, all fattening and loaded with sodium. There is also an entire row of organic munchies if you want to be healthy while you are eating unhealthy, but there is no compelling evidence that organic foods are any healthier than nonorganic foods, so you aren't any healthier for eating them, just paying more for the privilege. I visit the frozen food department and view the pizzas available. I count thirty-one varieties laden with all kinds of cheese, sausage, and salami, fully capable of clogging even the most intrepid artery. I maneuver my cart to the dairy cases where I select some Greek yogurt and some cheese slices for my dogs while eschewing the Ben & Jerry's Chunky Monkey. I pick up some more items for my recipe, and I'm on my way to the checkout line.

As I approach the end of my expedition, I carefully peruse the cash registers ahead, trying to decide which queue will move most quickly. I get behind the shortest line, but then I notice the little old lady at the front is writing a check out of her little old checkbook, and it takes her a full five minutes to make it out after she borrows a pen from the cashier, who needs to call her supervisor to receive approval. I make idle chitchat with the asthenic man ahead of me, and I can't help but notice that his cart contains the pretzels, chips, ice cream and frozen pizza that I had so carefully avoided on my sojourn. Finally the line moves again, but the next person has about ten coupons and the checker can't seem to scan them, and then there is a holdup while she again pages the supervisor. I resist the M&M's next to the checkout (placed there to test my willpower). At last I reach the counter and start placing my selections on the moving conveyor belt. I point out smugly that the brown balls are rutabaga as the cashier searches for the scanning code and gives me a disdainful glare. I whip out my credit card and give it a swipe, and then I'm asked if I approve the transaction. The stuff is ringing up at record pace and there is no way anyone can follow the rapidly expanding receipt, so of course I approve it. The teenage bagger asks me if I need help to my car. Do I look that old? As I push my cart loaded with provisions towards the exit, I suddenly feel a connection to the hunter-gatherers of prehistoric times. Now I just need to find my car in the parking lot.

My First Baseball Game

When I was five years old, my family moved to Chicago where my father began training as an ophthalmologist. The first televised baseball games occurred there, and the day contests of both the White Sox and Cubs were carried on WGNTV. Living on the south side of the city, I became an avid White Sox fan. Not only did I follow the team on TV, but I had my mother read me the box scores in the *Chicago Sun Times*. I soon learned to read the box scores myself. You can imagine my excitement when my father told me he had tickets for a game between the White Sox and the Yankees at Comiskey Park. (I was recently able to find the account of this game by going to www.baseballreference.com.)

It took place on June 3, 1953. My parents accompanied me to Sears Roebuck (the Roebuck was dropped many years ago) a few days before the game and bought me a White Sox uniform and a cap. I have an old picture of me wearing the cap, but not the uniform. I never understood how anyone would pick White Sox for the name of a team. As far as I can tell, it's the only sports team anywhere that has "white" in its name. The team came into the league as the White Stockings, well before drag queens, and the name was shortened to Sox. Even more baffling is that the Boston Americans changed their name to the Red Sox. Couldn't they at least have chosen caps, shirts, or pants?

I was so excited about my first game that I couldn't sleep, dreaming about a White Sox victory—I hated the Yankees, even at that tender age. My dad and I went to the park in his 1952 Chevrolet. I don't remember my sister or mother being present. In those days, it was mostly a male crowd. A policeman directed us to park in the front yard of someone's house, and we were instructed to leave ten dollars on the front seat. That was a way for the cops to get extra money in those days.

When I first saw the playing field, I was awed by the vivid hues, having only seen the playing field on black and white TV. The emerald green of the grass had been reproduced as a dull gray on television. The White Sox uniforms were actually a cream color, not the dull white I had imagined. We sat on the first base side of home plate. In the old stadiums, there were pillars holding up the stands, and if you sat behind one, you couldn't see the action too well. We weren't behind one, so I had an excellent view—a view I was soon to regret.

The Yankees were a great team in those days. They had won four World Series in a row and were about to win their fifth that year. Casey Stengel was the manager. He was a character who entertained the media with his wit. "Never make predictions, especially about the future." "Good pitching always stops good hitting and vice versa." Yogi Berra was on the team, and at the time, he was the best catcher in baseball. It was only years later that he passed Stengel in malapropisms. Mickey Mantle was in his third year and becoming a superstar. The White Sox had not won a World Series since 1917, and their last appearance had been in 1919, when several players admitted to taking money from gamblers to intentionally lose some games, the so-called Black Sox scandal. In the early 1950s they were mediocre, finishing third most years. Paul Richards was the manager. He was known for his kerfuffles with the umpires and had the distinction of being thrown out of more ballgames than any other manager in history.

Whitey Ford was pitching for the Yankees. He was in his early years and had just come back from a two-year hitch in Korea. Unlike today's pampered athletes, many of the players served in that war or WWII. He was 5-0 coming into the game and would go on to win eighteen that year. He was inducted into the Hall of Fame in 1974. I was hoping to see the Sox's ace Billy Pierce, and my dad liked Saul Rogovin, the only Jewish player on the team, but the White Sox pitcher this day was journeyman Bob Keegan. He had one great year in the major leagues; unfortunately 1953 was not that year. All the players on both teams were white, except for the Chicago left fielder, Minnie Minoso. The Yankees would not have a black player on their roster for another two years (Elston Howard).

The Yanks batted in the first inning. Keegan got the first batter out, but a walk and four singles later they led 3-0. Ford put down the Sox in the bottom of that inning. I knew all the statistics on each Sox player by heart and loudly announced them to my dad. The people around us were quite amazed as this little kid in a White Sox uniform spewed out the data. But the Yankees pushed across two more in the second, and Keegan headed to the shower, although he was still pretty clean, having retired only four batters.

The rout came in the fourth, when they scored five more. We were barely in our seats and it was 10-0! Here it was my first game, and the worst nightmare in my short life could not match this disaster. My dad bought me a hot dog, but the bun tasted like cardboard, and the kosher meat languished in my little stomach. The debacle continued, and we departed during the seventh-inning stretch when it was 17-2. I was spared the final humiliating Yankee run in the eighth. On the way home, we stopped for an ice cream cone, and I started to feel a little less despondent. I told my dad, "Billy Pierce is pitching tomorrow. Maybe they'll win that one!" They lost 9-5.

I never went to another game that year, and the following season, we moved away. Since then, I've been to many sporting events, but as I get older I prefer to watch most of them on television. I now have a high-definition flat screen TV, as opposed to the little black-and-white Motorola that we had in Chicago. I have a remote, so I can lie on the couch and switch to a cable news channel if the contest is a blowout. I don't know if it was my first game or my first disappointment, but the memory of that day has never left me. Although my favorite team had lost and I was dejected, I knew that my family still loved me, and there was always the hope of tomorrow. As for the White Sox, there was the next day, the next year, and even the next fifty-two years, for it took that long for the team to win another World Series after I attended that game, but by then I had become a Cardinals fan.

The Fabulous Fortune of Dr. Schmaltz

Dr. Leonard Schmaltz was a pretty average gastroenterologist; in fact he may have been a bit below average. He hadn't distinguished himself with any scientific publications, nor had he ever been a doctor to the rich and famous, and the high nasal tone of his voice and slight lisp considerably limited his bedside manner. However, he had one uncanny ability, and that was his prowess as an investor. Schmaltz hadn't taken any courses in business or economics, yet he had done careful calculations and determined that he had octupled his assets over the past twenty-five years. When he boasted about his financial wizardry to his colleagues in the doctors' lounge, they stared at him in amazement that such an obviously mediocre talent could be so fiscally successful.

When Dr.Schmaltz was beginning his practice, he hired an accountant and asked him where to invest his earnings. He was told that CD's were safe and paid five percent interest. This didn't sound right to him, and he told his advisor that if CD's were paying this rate, then AB's should be that much better. After the embarrassment of that foolish comment, he concluded that he needed to learn more about managing his money and purchased a subscription to the *Wall Street Journal*, which came to his house every morning.

In those early days he would carefully peruse each issue, then place the paper in the bottom of his pet hamster's (Bernie) cage to collect his excretions. He started reading about the monthly contest that would pit professional equity selections against a random choice by darts flung at the *Journal's* stock tables, and he noted with surprise that the darts would often beat the experts' picks. Schmaltz then devised a much more sophisticated process using his gastroenterologist's knowledge of mammalian feces. Every time he would clean Bernie's cage, he would take note of the placement of his droppings on the pages, and that would determine his stock pick.

Unbelievably his first selection was Microsoft which was selling for five dollars a share. He knew nothing about software, but what did he need to know? Bernie had made the fecal anointment, and that was good enough for him. He held the security until it rose to sixty dollars, and then he sold it. There was only one problem. Some of the poop clung to the stock listed right above it, Microshaft, an entity that made crankshafts for the mini Yugo that had just come on the market. Regrettably he threw a whole bunch of money at that one before it went bellyup, but because there was more excrement on the Microsoft than on the Microshaft, he only counted the gains that he had realized in the Microsoft acquisition and omitted the loss in the motor company.

In early 2000, he determined that the internet would be his next speculation. Again, he looked to his hamster Bernie in conjunction with the *Wall Street Journal* for guidance. He found a small corporation called Rodents.com, which had just gone public. For a small fee this online outfit would deliver the animal of choice to your door. If you needed some porcupines for a native headdress, a rabbit for a stew, a ground hog to celebrate Groundhog Day, or some rats to study the bubonic plague, they could be obtained at one all-encompassing critter conglomerate. The stock rocketed out of the gate, and before he knew it, he was up threefold from his initial investment. He called his broker about selling his position and was told to think about it overnight and call the next morning.

At the Passover Seder that evening, he sat next to his obnoxious brother-in-law Bernie (no relation to the hamster), who was a veterinarian. In the midst of the four cups of wine, he mentioned that there was a strong demand from all the snake owners in his practice for live mice to feed to their pet pythons, and the tastiest gnawers could only be obtained from Rodents.com. Schmaltz couldn't believe the coincidence! This stock was going to explode through the roof, but he kept this knowledge to himself; he didn't'want that jerk of a relative in on the deal. He called his broker the next day and told him not to sell but to buy more.

About three days later, he noticed in the *Journal* that the price of the security was starting to fall. Never fear, he thought to himself, this is a slam dunk. He continued to buy. He doubled and then tripled down on his stake. Then the bad news hit. A civil war had erupted in East Tumboko where all the delectable mice had been raised, and the company could no longer obtain these animals. The shares went down faster than the spheres that Galileo had dropped from the leaning tower of Pisa.

The next Passover, he had his annual dinner with Bernie and the ignoramus bragged about how he had shorted Rodents.com after he read in the *National Geographic* that there might be tribal unrest in East Tumboko over burial rights near the Kakakulugoo River. Twelve years later, Schmaltz's lawsuit against his broker is still winding its way through the legal morass, but he continues to mark the stock at its peak value, believing that he will eventually be reimbursed that amount by the courts.

In the middle of the last decade, the Warren Buffet of gastroenterology deduced that real estate was a great place to park his money. The butt practice was going well, and he decided to invest in a shopping center. His other brother-in-law, Murray, was a real estate agent, and he recommended a midsized operation with two great anchor stores, Circuit City and Borders Books. The cash flow was unbelievable, and Schmaltz resolved to buy out his other three partners. Today the center is mostly vacant except for Kim's Korean Dry Cleaners, which is doing a brisk business. Murray and Dr. Schmaltz are in litigation, but he is gratified that he no longer receives an invitation to attend the Seder with his wife's family, and there will be tax write-offs into the future as far as the eye can see.

Six months ago the Schmaltz's were at the mall, and they

tried out a fantastic bed in The Sleep Store. Even though it was very expensive, they chose to acquire the product, and when it arrived at their home, it exceeded even their highest expectations. Schmaltz analyzed the firm mattress firm and decided to purchase its stock. Several weeks later, the price started to deteriorate due to an earnings shortfall related to competition from cheap knock-offs, but he had learned his lesson and sold his shares before they reached half of his initial investment. Schmaltz anticipates that the company will be going bust, but he is certain that someday their mattress will be a collector's item, so he is not declaring a loss at this time.

The good doctor always planned to retire at the age of sixty-five and begin spending his considerable nest egg, but as he approaches that milestone, the practice of gastroenterology has suddenly become much more appealing to him. He now realizes that he would greatly miss the four a.m. phone call from the patient with constipation, the office visit of the bloated individual who can't fart, or the diagnostic challenge of the middle-aged woman with excessive belching. He would be bored on the Fourth of July if he couldn't leave his family's celebration for the trip to the emergency room to remove impacted barbecue from some unfortunate fellow's esophagus. No, he has resolved to keep cleaning out colons, probably until the age of ninety-five, not because he has to, but because he wants to. In the meantime, he's convinced that yak's milk is the next hot commodity, and he has taken a substantial position in an Inner Mongolian dairy company.

Hippocrates and Ms. Payne

I first encountered Ms. Dolores Payne last year, when she came to the office for a second opinion regarding her abdominal pain. She had been under the care of another gastroenterologist, but her symptoms hadn't improved, and she had recently been hospitalized where the usual battery of tests had been negative. As I took her history, I could see that she had a worried, painful look on her countenance. She described excruciating lower abdominal pain radiating around to her back, accompanied by alternating diarrhea and constipation. When the pain was at its worst, she had uncontrolled vomiting as well. I came to the conclusion that Ms. Payne was suffering from irritable bowel syndrome.

A clue to our poor understanding of the condition is attested to by the word "irritable." There are no diseases such as grouchy heart, irascible lung, petulant pancreas, or cantankerous kidney. Only the gut has a mood disorder. I made some dietary modifications, started her on belladonna, and reassured her that her condition was not serious and that she should expect resolution of her problem over the next few months. She seemed very appreciative of my assessment, and promised to follow the regimen that I had prescribed. I felt quite satisfied with my performance, and fully anticipated that she would return in three weeks, feeling much improved. I could not have been more misguided.

One night I received a call from the emergency room physician. Ms. Payne had arrived with her usual constellation of complaints, and he was admitting her to the hospital. When I saw her the next morning, she had the same lugubrious face, and her lower abdomen was tender to palpation, but unchanged since I had seen her in the office. My treatment had not worked, and if anything, she felt worse. That afternoon, her hospitalist contacted me. He thought that the correct diagnosis could have been missed on her previous admission, and he was ordering a new series of tests, which, of course, came back normal. Her symptoms became more tolerable, I stopped the intravenous morphine, and she was discharged. Ten days later, she was back in the emergency room and convinced a different doctor that she needed to be readmitted. I consulted a surgical colleague who agreed that there was no indication for an operation. A psychiatrist saw her and suggested an antidepressant. This time I knew that my previous regimen was a failure, and I changed her medications.

She returned to the office a few weeks later. When I saw her name on the examining room door, an anxious feeling came over me. What if Ms. Payne was no better? I gently opened the door and tiptoed into the room. I took one look at her face, a face contorted with anguish and agony, and I knew that I had failed. Over the course of the next few months, I tried every treatment in my armamentarium. I prescribed all the antis: antispasmodics, antacids, antibiotics, and antiemetics (I would have tried antipasto if I thought it could work). I then switched to the pros: probiotics, promotility agents, and Protonix. Nothing helped. Finally, I confessed to her that my treatment had been completely unsuccessful. I suggested that she seek another opinion, although there was a six-month wait to see a university consultant. Ms. Payne seemed dismayed by my admission of failure and replied that I was a good doctor who was giving my best effort, and she still wanted to be my patient. Even though this kind of gratitude is what doctors thrive on, my inner voice was howling: *No! No! No!*

I arrived home that night in a despondent mood, thinking about the bleak prospect of treating Ms. Payne for the remainder of my medical career. I nagged at my wife and barked at the dog. I turned on the TV and started mindlessly flipping the channels. I flossed my teeth and stumbled into bed, expecting a restless night with visions of Dolores Payne interrupting my sleep.

Suddenly, I was in ancient Greece, and, to my astonishment, I was in a group of acolytes listening to a lecture from Hippocrates himself. He looked at me and asked, "who are you?" I replied, "Margolis, sir, from the 21 century."

"Oh, is that a Greek name?"

"No, sir, Jewish."

"Well, what do you want, Margolis?"

"I came to ask you about my patient Dolores Payne, whom I can't get well." I proceeded to present her story. As I was talking, Hippocrates had a pensive look and after I had finished, he began to speak. "I commend you for your detailed history, but I don't understand all of the silly tests that you performed; totally unnecessary. It's clear that she has imbalance of the four humors."

"The four humors?" I asked.

"Yes the human body consists of four substances: blood, yellow bile, black bile, and phlegm. Don't they teach that anymore? Your patient has too much black bile coming from the spleen, and that's causing her melancholy and bad temper. I suggest an herbal regimen of white hellebore, thapsian, and cucumber juice to restore that balance. If that fails, some daucke or cuckoo-pint might help." I awoke startled and looked at the clock; it was two a.m.

My eyes closed, and I resumed my dream. I was in Rome in the second century and in the presence of Galen, one of the greatest physicians who ever lived. As I told my sorry tale, the august man fidgeted with his toga, and his eyes squinted at me. He interrupted me about halfway into my presentation. "Did you take her pulse? I have written sixteen books on the pulse. The pulse originates from the arteries, and it pumps the red blood that's made in the heart. The dark venous blood has no pulse, and, of course, that's made in the liver. There's no doubt that she has more dark blood than red blood, and because she is a Virgo, I suggest some theriac tonic consisting of ground-up lizard and viper flesh, along with some moist clay, spices, and herbs, and I would apply the leeches daily." I slumbered on, and soon I was in Philadelphia in the eighteenth century, and I was discussing Ms. Payne with Dr. Benjamin Rush, the famous physician and signer of the Declaration of Independence. After hearing my story, he told me that the cure was obvious. "Bleed her until she faints, and then purge her with large doses of calomel (mercurous chloride now known to be toxic to the human body)."

The next thing I knew, it was morning. I mulled over my dream and was thankful to be alive in the current century, knowing that the ancients were clueless in their treatments. I got dressed and drove to work, but I couldn't stop thinking of Hippocrates. When I arrived at my office, I opened the bottom drawer of my desk and found an old copy of the Hippocratic Oath that I had kept since medical school. I started to read. My eyes drifted down to the fourth line, "I will remember that there is art to medicine as well as science, and that warmth, sympathy, and understanding may outweigh the surgeon's knife or the chemist's drug." I immediately realized that this was a role that physicians have played since the beginning of civilization. Even in our technologic age, we don't have all the answers. Maybe fifty or a hundred years from now, my antis and pros will be as laughable as cuckoo-pint or theriac tonic, but we can still sit in the examining room, put down our computers, listen to our patients, and try to give them comfort.

I recently saw Ms. Payne in the office. As far as I could tell, she hadn't improved, but we talked about our children and grandchildren and our hopes for their future, and she seemed less anxious and a little more optimistic when the visit ended. She went to the check-out desk and made another appointment. She will be coming back in three weeks.

The Life and Times of an Imaginary Friend

My name is Joe, and for most of my ethereal existence, I have worked as an imaginary friend. My father, Manny, was a goblin but was forced into retirement after suffering war wounds fighting the leprechauns, and he currently receives a pension as a hobbled goblin. My mother, Ethel, was a pixie (not to be confused with fairy) who emigrated from England with the Pilgrims. After playing pranks on unsuspecting children for many centuries, she settled down with Manny, and I was produced in a cauldron. As my mother pulled me from the boiling brew, I emitted a muffled whimper, not a forceful cry, and she knew immediately that I would not be a wizard or a sorcerer or even a gnome, but I would have to find work as a make-believe chum.

In the early 1950s, the depression and world wars had ended, and kids had more leisure time. Television was in its infancy, and playmates weren't always available, so they turned to mythical companions to fill out their day. My first employer was Dave from Canada. Dave was eight years old when I first went to work for him. He was an avid sports fan who believed that he was destined to be a professional athlete. I spent much of my employment as his opponent in fantasy sport contests that we played in his bedroom, and like the Harlem Globetrotters and the Washington Generals, I was on the losing end ninety-nine percent of the time.

He was afraid of the dark, and I remember numerous scuffles with the monsters in his bedroom closet. Dave had a vivid imagination, and several other fictional buddies vied for his attention. He had a favorite shirt named Favey (the subject of a previous story) who was more of a daytime pal, but we often competed with each other when Dave came home from school. I have to admit that he was one dude who rubbed me the wrong way, even though he was made of a soft flannel. There were some other competitors as well: Fluffy the blanket, Cuddly the rabbit, and Goldie the Crayola crayon.

Things pretty much stayed this way until Dave reached puberty. I noticed a change when Lola first appeared. It seems that Dave had gotten hold of a *Playboy* magazine in which Lola had been in the centerfold, and it wasn't long before she joined the rest of us on the imaginary team. Soon Dave was spending most of his free time with Lola behind a locked bathroom door. When I asked him about his activities in the lavatory, he was very evasive. I queried Fluffy and Cuddly, but they were clueless. Favey ignored my questions, but it was obvious that he was also in the dark.

One day Dave's mother came into the bedroom and took the blanket and rabbit away, and I heard her tell Dave's dad that they had been donated to charity. Favey became too small for Dave to wear and joined the rag pile. Several weeks went by, and Dave stopped playing our sports games, and I knew my tenure was coming to an end. One day I discovered that Lola had occupied my usual space in Dave's cerebral cortex, and I found myself in the hippocampus where a neuron brusquely notified me that I was terminated. No surprise retirement party or tearful goodbye from Dave. I headed out into the cosmos as a UIF (unemployed imaginary friend).

While out in the ether space, I visited the Wizard, hoping that he could find me a job. He informed me that the buddy market was slow, but harpies, werewolves, griffins, and trolls were in demand. Unfortunately he didn't think I was wicked enough to qualify for any of those occupations.

In the meantime, he suggested seasonal employment at the North Pole as a temporary elf. I started work tending to the reindeer; all the toy making was done by the permanent staff. Rudolph was the rock star of the group, but close up his red nose looked more like a bad case of rosacea. My job was to hitch the animals to the sleigh when Santa came by for practice runs. One day Blitzen kicked me in the groin, and I knew that the elf occupation was not for me.

Shortly after that, I found work with a five-year-old boy in Pennsylvania named Billy. The *Star Wars* movies were popular then, and his parents took him to all of the episodes, but he had terrifying dreams afterwards. I spent many nighttime hours tussling with Darth Vader and trying to soothe Billy's fears. Although there were no other imaginary companions, Billy spent much of his day glued to the television watching *Sesame Street*. I was no match for Elmo or Bert and Ernie, so it was a rather lonely existence in the cerebrum. When Billy was about ten years old, his nightmares suddenly evaporated and I was again unemployed. I drifted to Hollywood, hoping that there might be a need for a supernatural character. I auditioned for *Ghostbusters, Poltergeist*, and even for the Freddy Krueger character, but never landed a part. I was probably too congenial to be a scary ghost, and the friendly roles were already locked up by Casper.

A few years ago, I was hired by Stevie, a six-year old who lived in San Diego. Stevie's mother and father were divorced, and he was constantly shuttling from one parent to another. They were busy professionals and didn't seem to have much time for Stevie. I was the fictional brother, and we spent countless hours talking about his mom and dad, longing for the time when they had been together. I didn't particularly like either parent, but I kept up a happy banter with Stevie during that difficult period.

On his twelfth birthday, he received an Xbox from his dad. After that Stevie became addicted to video games, and I drifted into the ether again. I started thinking wistfully about my first job with Dave so many years ago. The conflicts with Favey and Lola had faded, and even losing all those fictional games didn't seem so bad. I put my name in cyberspace at imaginaryfriends.com, trying to locate Dave.

Sure enough, a few weeks ago I was reunited with Dave, who is now sixty-five years old. To my surprise, he became a physician and has had a successful practice as a gastroenterologist for over thirty years. When I knew Dave as a kid, he seemed too unfocused and fidgety to make much of himself. He has written several short stories and even put me in one of them, although I hated to read that my arch rival Favey was the main character. I shuffled up to the cerebral cortex and had a look around. There were a lot more memories in there than on my first sojourn. Most were pleasurable, some were painful, and some were locked away and will never be retrieved. I slid down to the hippocampus and found the nasty neuron that had bumped me out so many years ago. He was now grizzled and still abrupt but seemed generally glad to see me. He told me that Lola had left a few years after me and had been replaced by Bridgette, then Rusty, and finally Gina.

Dave is no longer fearful of the dark, as I found out the first evening when he shouted at his wife to turn out the lights so he could sleep. The problem now is that he wakes up frequently, as people tend to do when they get old. When he is in the twilight zone between wakefulness and slumber, we talk about his childhood and the hopes and fears that we shared. He brags about his young grandchildren, and I help him remember his grandfather, who is now only a distant memory. I tell Dave that he will be funny and generous and caring, just like his grandfather was. I've learned that we all can't be wizards or sorcerers, and that a loyal and comforting friend is just as valuable.

Dave has reassured me that I will have a permanent home as long as he is alive, but someday I will ascend the gentle zephyr to the heavens, and from the top of some rainbow or on some distant star, I will look down at the earth hoping to join the fantasy of another child who will need me to help him cope with this complicated world.

Sarah

Dr. Joseph Goldstone was at the end of a long day. He had received several telephone calls during the night concerning a critical patient in the intensive care unit with a hemorrhaging ulcer and had debated with himself about getting dressed and driving back to the hospital, a thirty-minute drive from his home, to have another look in the fellow's stomach. Fortunately, he was able to obtain a few more hours of fitful sleep before performing the gastroscopy at six-thirty a.m., ahead of his regularly scheduled procedures. He headed back to his office around noon and, after a quick hummus and pickle sandwich from home, began seeing his clinic patients. As he walked over to his desk to answer another call from the ICU, he glanced down at his patient list. The last name was a new consultation, Sarah Peebles, and her insurance was listed as Medicaid. In the state of Missouri, the Medicaid reimbursement was exceeding miserly and few physicians accepted it, particularly specialists. Dr. Goldstone was still developing his practice and had chosen to enroll in all of the health plans including Medicaid, but he also felt an ethical obligation to the poor, and so he was the only gastroenterologist in the area who accepted these luckless people. He noted that this one had been referred by Dr. Seth Jones who sent most of his business to Goldstone's rival, Nick Forsythe, but reserved his occasional Medicaid client for Goldstone, as Forsythe would not take those cases. This fact, as well as the long, exhausting day, had put Goldstone in a rather sour mood as he entered the examining room of Miss Peebles.

Sarah was a young African American female, seventeen years old, with a coppered-colored complexion, and if her darker-skinned mother had not been with her, he would have been confused as to her racial origin. She was thin, with auburn hair and striking brown eyes surrounded by dark circles of chronic illness. Sarah did most of the talking and did not seem put off by Goldstone's uncharacteristically abrupt manner. Sarah had been diagnosed with Crohn's disease about two years previously after developing severe diarrhea. She had been hospitalized in Nebraska where they resided, and the gastroenterologist there had started her on corticosteroids and anti-inflammatory medications. After her parents separated six months ago, she and her mother moved to Missouri to be closer to relatives until her mother could find a job. Sarah had plans to finish high school, attend college, and become a lawyer; the obvious frown on Goldstone's face unmasked his skepticism.

The disease had remitted, but absent health insurance and money, the young woman had stopped her medications after the move. Approximately three months ago, there was a reemergence of the symptoms, and she had lost ten pounds from her already bony frame. When her Medicaid became active, her aunt had suggested Dr. Jones, who had referred her to Goldstone. The tired physician glanced at his watch, then hurriedly ran through the remainder of the history and physical and scheduled Sarah for a colonoscopy later in the week. This examination revealed numerous whitish ulcers in the colon and small intestine consistent with the diagnosis of recurrent Crohn's disease. He related these finding to Sarah and her mother, and restarted the previous medications.

Six weeks later Sarah returned to the office, her symptoms markedly improved, but her home life was lamentable. She had not seen her father since leaving Nebraska, and her mother had filed for divorce; Mrs. Peebles was still unemployed, so they were dependent on food stamps. Her brave demeanor in the face of these hardships struck a chord within Goldstone, and he began to regret his rude manner on the first visit. He found himself talking about his own painful divorce. At that time, he was having difficulty seeing his two children who were around Sarah's age. His ex-wife had spent their college savings and had recently informed him that he would need to pay again, on top of the child support and alimony. Goldstone had been taught in medical school not to discuss your personal life with a patient, but over the years he had discovered that some individuals enjoyed his personal anecdotes, which displayed a human quality about the doctor that many individuals found comforting.

Sarah saw Goldstone intermittently and sometimes didn't

keep her appointments, as is often the case with young people who have chronic ailments. One day, Sarah arrived with her mother, whom he had not seen since the original encounter, and Goldstone knew that this was ominous news even before he walked into the room. Her main complaint was belly pain, which gripped her in spasms and lasted for several minutes. Goldstone palpated her abdomen, and she winced. For the first time, her sunny countenance had been replaced by the hurt and apprehension of this debilitating disease. When he listened with his stethoscope, he could hear the high-pitched bowel sounds indicative of a bowel obstruction. Goldstone had pulled out his order sheet for admission, when her mother broke further bad news. Because she had turned nineteen, Sarah had lost her Medicaid and again was without insurance. Goldstone contemplated the alternatives. He was about to advise Sarah and her mother to go to the emergency room of the university hospital in town and be done with her, but when he looked at the frightened, sickly girl, supine on the exam table, he changed his mind. Instead, he called the hospitalist at the local community hospital where he was on staff and told her that Sarah was coming in to be evaluated. Sure enough, a CT scan confirmed an obstruction.

After a few days of high-dose steroids, it was obvious that the blockage was not improving, and the hospitalist requested the surgeon on call for a consultation. Dr. Morris examined Sarah and agreed that she needed an operation, but he thought it too complex for him to perform, and he recommended transfer to a teaching institution. When Goldstone heard this he became irate, as he knew from previous experience that the surgery was often routine, and he suspected that her lack of health coverage was influencing Morris' decision to punt. He called his good friend Michael Reynolds, an excellent surgeon, and asked him for a favor. He explained Sarah's predicament, and Reynolds agreed to perform the surgery for free. Sarah had three feet of her small intestine and part of her colon removed, but she made an excellent recovery, and was discharged six days later. Goldstone visited her daily and was pleased that Sarah had quickly regained her positive outlook and almost inappropriate cheerfulness.

The surgery solved the problem for a while, and he didn't see Sarah again until she came to the office with a minor flare-up five years later. He was impressed that she was in her second year of law school, and he remembered his cynicism about her goals on their first meeting. Goldstone mentioned that he had remarried, and recently returned from a Scandinavian cruise, but he was discreet enough not to tell her about an ugly lawsuit that had shaken his confidence and caused him to sleep poorly at night, even without the phone calls. Once again, he chalked up this visit to charity and postponed plans for a repeat colonoscopy, for even if he waived his professional fee, the hospital, anesthesia, and pathology bills would run over one thousand dollars, and how would her mother pay for that? Goldstone restarted the medication, which fortunately was a less-expensive generic, and sent Sarah home.

One afternoon, Sarah returned, pale and gaunt. Immediately Goldstone knew that the Crohn's had resurfaced, but despite her disability, she appeared happy to see her old doctor. She had passed the bar exam and was working in the city as a prosecuting attorney, and of course she now had medical coverage.

As usual, she inquired into Goldstone's situation, more as a friend than a patient. Goldstone rambled on and on about his children, his new wife, the modern-day realities of medicine, and his difficulty coping with the computer age. Another colonoscopy confirmed his suspicions, and he suggested one of the newer biologic agents that had just been approved for Crohn's disease. Sarah was no longer living in the area, so he arranged for her to receive the intravenous medication at a clinic near her home. She called him a couple of weeks later to tell him that the drug had produced a dramatic effect, and she was feeling back to normal. She had talked to the nurse at the infusion center who had recommended one of their doctors, and she had decided to switch to him because of his location. Goldstone was disappointed but not surprised. He had seen Sarah when she was poor and lacked insurance, and now that she had become successful, she had switched physicians, but he was gratified that she had responded so well to the treatment that he had prescribed.

Time went by, and after forty years in practice, Goldstone had slowed down considerably. The part of town where he worked had changed, now populated with mostly poor immigrants and African Americans, with the whites taking flight and moving further into the suburbs, aided by the construction of one super freeway after another. Now the charity and Medicaid patients took up more of his practice, along with the elderly population that had stayed in their original homes. Once he came to work to find police cars surrounding the building and was told that thieves had broken into the neighboring dentist's office. He developed glaucoma and a slight tremor of his left hand, so he decided to stop performing gastroscopies and colonoscopies before his skill severely diminished. Finally, at age seventy, he decided not to take on any new patients, but because of decreased reimbursements, he soon recognized that the practice had become a losing proposition and he set a retirement date.

Ultimately, the appointed day arrived. Goldstone woke up that morning and put on his usual white shirt, slightly stained tie, and rumpled sports jacket; clothing he knew he would never wear again except at weddings and funerals—possibly his own. He slumped into his car and took the last drive to his office, and said hello to his faithful nurse for the last time. He only had a few patients to see and spent most of that time reminiscing with them about how they had first met, their retirement plans, and their kids. They seemed genuinely sad to see him go.

Unexpectedly there was a commotion outside of the building. A police car had pulled up along with a black SUV. Goldstone thought to himself: Just my luck, trouble on my terminal day of work. He went out to the waiting room to determine the cause of the disturbance and was perplexed when a woman dressed in a fashionable business suit, accompanied by several assistants, walked into the office. Suddenly Goldstone realized that Sarah had come back to see him in his final hour. She ran up to the elderly physician and gave him a prolonged hug and a kiss on the cheek which surprised her entourage. She looked behind her and an aide handed her a wooden plaque with gold-plated lettering. She gave it to Goldstone, who read the inscription. "To Dr. Joseph Goldstone in recognition of his long service to his patients, regardless of their status in life, their race, or their ability to pay, and for taking care of me all these years, Sarah Peebles, Attorney General of the State of Missouri." As Goldstone read, he became choked and unable to speak, but as he groped for words to thank her, a revelation surfaced from deep in his soul: in the end, his life had counted. A tear rolled down his wrinkled cheek.

Turning Sixty-Five

I woke with a start after I had an attack
Of pain, which settled deep in my back.
Down in the sacrum or one of the lumbar,
Do I need a scan to find out the number?
But now I remember when I got up to pee,
I looked at the clock; it was a quarter to three.
And on the way back, still partly asleep,
I tripped over the dog and went down in a heap.
So maybe the ache I perceive in my spine,
Is only a bruise where my bones hit the pine?

And that wrench in my elbow; it could be bursitis,
Fibromyalgia, or even arthritis.
The left hand today seems slightly numb,
Most likely related to the twitch in my thumb.
But the pounding throb that shoots through my head
Could be a stroke, and that's what I dread.
And the continuous ringing that I have in my ears,
And my persistent dry eyes without any tears,
And despite frequent flossing I have a bad gum,
So no wonder this morning I feel a bit glum.

Sometimes I sense a pressure deep in my chest,
For who knows what's brewing under my breast?
Are the coronaries plugged? Is the heart muscle flaccid?
Or is the pain, simply reflux of acid?
And the skips in my heart that come after dinner,
Will I need a pacemaker or just a blood thinner?
The occasional cough is probably a spasm,
But I can't rule out an occult neoplasm.
So I lie in the bed afraid to get up,
Fearful my organs just won't hold up.

Did I already mention my trips to the toilet?
My passage is rusted, I wish I could oil it.
And I have constant bloating and abdominal distention,
I produce enough gas to run a small engine.
I open my eyes and look up with a stare,
At nothing in general, only the air.
But all at once my face starts to flush,
Not from a fever but a rapturous rush.
And suddenly I realize I needn't despair,
For today is the first day I'll receive Medicare!

About the Author

Dr. David Margolis practiced gastroenterology in St. Louis for thirty-six years before retiring in 2013. His stories have appeared in several medical journals as well as on HumorPress.com, *Long Story Short* and *Still Crazy*. He resides in Creve Coeur, MO with his wife, two poodles, and a set of golf clubs.

www.ingramcontent.com/pod-product-compliance
Lightning Source LLC
Chambersburg PA
CBHW070534100726
47907CB00004B/1108